Darrin smiled as the thrill of the chase gathered, began trickling through his veins.

He slipped several eight-by-ten color photographs from a manila envelope and began studying them, though he no longer needed them to call up the image of Emily Kampion.

It was an exquisite face—fair skinned, oval. The platinum-blond hair was natural, according to the information in the file. Delicate features, clearly defined. The blue eyes were large and dark. The mouth, with its full, faintly pouting lower lip, stopped just short of being too wide.

A beautiful woman. An intelligent, potentially dangerous woman.

He was finally going to see her in the flesh. He had to make careful plans for meeting her, getting to know her. The lady was shrewd—she'd managed to elude the FBI for a full year—so whatever plan he worked out had to be perfect.

The dark eyes stared challengingly at him. She would be a worthy opponent.

"It should be interesting, Mrs. Kampion," he murmured, slipping the photographs back into the envelope.

Dear Reader,

Once again we have a lineup of compelling, passionate and impossible-to-put-down books for you. If excitement is the hallmark of Silhouette Intimate Moments, you'll find lots of it this month.

Lee Magner's *Sutter's Wife* was especially well-received when it was published last spring. Now Grant Macklin, introduced to readers in that book, has a story—and a romance—of his own. In *The Dragon's Lair*, he meets a woman who is his perfect complement, but neither one of them may live long enough to achieve "happily ever after" unless they can catch the killer stalking them. Jeanne Stephens's *Hiding Places* proves once again why its author is so highly regarded by those who like a little suspense mixed with their romance. The lush island setting of St. Thomas is deceptive, for it is against this seemingly peaceful background that a life-and-death drama is played out for Darrin Boyle and the woman he knows as Cathy Prentiss. Round out the month with Marilyn Cunningham's *Enchanted Circle*, a tale of centuries-old rituals with the power to threaten today, and Linda Turner's *Moonlight and Lace*, a story of two people who are given a second chance to find the love they missed the first time around.

In months to come, look for new books by Emilie Richards, Linda Shaw, Barbara Faith and all the other authors who make Silhouette Intimate Moments so special.

Leslie J. Wainger
Senior Editor and Editorial Coordinator

JEANNE STEPHENS

Hiding Places

SILHOUETTE·INTIMATE·MOMENTS®

Published by Silhouette Books New York

America's Publisher of Contemporary Romance

SILHOUETTE BOOKS
300 East 42nd St., New York, N.Y. 10017

ISBN: 0-373-07353-4

First Silhouette Books printing October 1990

Printed in the U.S.A.

JEANNE STEPHENS

loves to travel, but she's always glad to get home to Oklahoma. This incurable romantic and mother of three loves reading ("I'll read anything!" she says), needlework, photography, long walks, during which she works out her latest books, and, of course, her own romantic hero: her husband.

Chapter 1

When the telephone rang, he was standing, naked, in front of the open refrigerator. He was contemplating making a sandwich from the remains of a baked ham. Instead, he grabbed a beer, flipped the tab and took a long swallow. On the way to the phone, he glanced at the red numerals on the range clock.

Midnight. An hour ago, he'd left a party early—to the clear disappointment of the hostess. Bored beyond words, he had found it impossible to engage in further social chitchat. Not that his ennui was the fault of his hostess or the other guests. Its cause was in himself.

He'd savored the short walk home through quiet Georgetown streets, the air stung by the chill of autumn, hoping the exercise would quiet the restlessness that had dogged him for several months, ever since he'd been assigned to the Kampion case. It hadn't. The case was stalled, had been since before he'd taken it on. He had other cases, of course, but this one nagged him.

Sometimes, like now, he wondered if he'd get another full night's sleep until Frank Kampion was behind bars.

The ringing of the telephone at midnight created a spark of hope that, for the moment at least, pushed the restiveness down. He strode through the dark apartment to his bedroom, where the tangled sheets gave evidence to his futile attempts at sleep. Setting the beer on the bedside table, he switched on a lamp beside which rested a telephone, several pens and a memo pad.

Ignoring the phone that was in plain sight, he reached for the one concealed behind a sliding panel in the oak storage unit that formed the bed's pier headboard. The number of the concealed phone was unlisted, known to only a handful of people, and the line was checked for taps at frequent intervals. When the phone had been installed upon his arrival in Washington, he'd found it amusing, like something in a superspy film. He'd since come to appreciate the better-safe-than-sorry caution.

"This is Boyle."

"Rainey." The familiar voice was rough with the chain-smoker's raspiness.

"Past your bedtime, isn't it?" It was well-known at the bureau that Rainey and his wife retired at 10:00 p.m., like clockwork. If you disturbed him after that, you'd better have something vitally important to say.

Rainey ignored the rhetorical question. "One of our men spotted a woman who looks like Emily Kampion—with brown hair." Rainey wasted no time on polite preliminaries. Boyle had once tried to picture Rainey dispensing idle chatter at a cocktail party but his imagination boggled at the attempt.

He reached for the frosty beer can. "What man?" He lifted the can and swallowed.

"Zenke, stationed in New Orleans. Seasoned agent. Know him?"

"I've heard the name."

"He's plodding but dependable."

"What the hell is New Orleans doing in this? It's my case."

"Don't get territorial, Boyle." Wryness tinged the scratchy voice before a cough rattled over the line. "A minute," he gasped and coughed again.

He sipped his beer and waited.

Rainey went on, "The sighting's a coincidence. Blind luck, if it turns out to be anything but another false lead. Zenke's registered at a hotel in Charlotte Amalie. Vacation."

"St. Thomas?"

"Yeah, that surprised me, too. I expected them to head for Brazil, some safe haven like that. New York—Chicago, at least—if they were brave enough to remain in the country. But the Virgin Islands? Reverse psychology, maybe."

"What about Kampion?"

"He's not been sighted. Zenke's hotel is near the apartment building where the woman is living. He spotted her twice, but she's been alone both times. If Kampion's there, he's staying inside."

"Did Zenke see the child?"

"Negative. But if the woman is our quarry with dyed hair or a wig, the kid's around somewhere. And if Kampion is in that apartment, he has to come out eventually."

"If he isn't with them at the moment, he'll show up sooner or later."

"I'd put a year's salary on it."

"I'll leave as soon as I can book a flight."

"It's covered. Tomorrow, 5:45 a.m. out of International. Pick up your ticket at the American desk. I'll inform the D.C. office, have your other cases temporarily reassigned."

He scribbled the flight time and name of the airline as Rainey talked. "Got it. Did Zenke find out what she calls herself?"

"Catherine Prentiss. Well, that's it. Oh, and Boyle, don't go off on one of your damned solo tangents." He coughed. "Check in as soon as you're located in Charlotte Amalie."

"I know the drill, Rainey."

"That's never been in question," said the other man sardonically.

"Go to bed, old man. And trash those cigarettes before they trash you."

"There's no zealot quite as self-righteous as a reformed nicotine addict," Rainey growled.

He smiled, hung up and slid the concealing panel back in place. He tipped the can and finished the beer. The thrill of the chase gathered, began trickling through his veins. He took a high curving hook shot with the empty can and hit the wastebasket dead-on.

He lifted a suitcase from the closet shelf and packed with an economy of movement developed through frequent practice over the past eight years. Ten minutes later, his packing finished, he returned to the closet for his attaché case and a portable computer and printer in compact carrying cases.

He found the latest packet mailed to him by his brother, Kent, and transferred two manuscript printouts to the attaché case. This was one of the occasions when his most frequent cover as a writer—for which he'd been briefed by Kent, the real writer in the family—would be perfect. The manuscripts were computer books, Kent's latest output. His brother always sent copies of his completed manuscripts, finding his "contributions to national security" endlessly amusing.

Before closing the attaché case, he added a supply of ammunition to the automatic concealed in the shallow space beneath the false bottom of the case. After replacing the false bottom, he slipped several eight-by-ten color photographs from a manila envelope and studied them, even though he no longer needed them to call up the image of Emily Kampion. Lately she'd starred in most of his dreams. Unpleasant dreams in which he was being shot at or shoved from speeding cars. He always had bad dreams when he was waiting for developments in a case. The inactivity made him crazy.

Emily Kampion's face was exquisite—fair skinned, oval. Her platinum blond hair was natural, according to the information in her file. Delicate features, the nose short and straight, the cheekbones clearly defined. Her blue eyes were large, so dark they appeared to be the color of the navy suit he'd laid out for the flight. Her mouth, with its full, faintly pouting bottom lip, stopped just short of being too wide.

A beautiful woman. An intelligent, potentially dangerous woman.

He hoped Zenke was right, that he was finally going to see her in the flesh. If he agreed with the New Orleans agent that she could be Kampion's wife, he'd begin with laying careful plans for meeting her, getting to know her. The lady was shrewd—she'd managed to elude the FBI for a full year—so whatever plan he worked out would have to be nonthreatening. And what could be more innocuous than an author of technical books?

The dark blue eyes stared at him from the photographs, challenging him. She would be a worthy opponent.

"It should be interesting, Mrs. Kampion," he muttered and slipped the photographs back into the envelope.

He hesitated a moment, then removed the false bottom again and tucked in the photographs with the automatic and ammunition.

He set the computer, printer and attaché case next to his suitcase and, once more, felt a rush of vitality with its hairline edge of excitement. The feeling came when an investigation was finally moving forward after being stalled for a period of time. He wouldn't let himself entertain the thought that the trail he was following to St. Thomas might well end in another dead end.

He could sleep now. He set the alarm for 4:00 a.m., snapped off the light, and crawled between the sheets.

Cathy opened the French doors and stepped out onto the flagstone terrace, leaving one door ajar so that she could hear Angel when she woke from her nap. During the seven months they'd spent in Houston, Angel had had frequent nightmares. Although the dreams had diminished greatly in the five months since they'd arrived in St. Thomas, once in a while she still awoke terrified, sobbing that the monsters were trying to get her.

Cathy felt guilty about the nightmares. She had been so careful never to say anything critical about Frank in Angel's hearing. In fact, she never mentioned him to

Angel at all, except to attempt satisfactory answers to her questions about her father. Not always an easy task.

The questions had been frequent the first few weeks, but Angel hadn't asked about Frank for months now. From what Cathy could tell, the child had no memory of the life they'd led until a year ago on the secluded estate outside San Francisco. Angel had been only two when they left, so naturally whatever memories she'd carried away with her had faded quickly.

But children sensed things. The nightmares seemed to Cathy proof that she hadn't been completely successful at hiding her own fear from her daughter. Thank goodness children were resilient. Angel hadn't had a nightmare in about seven weeks now.

As for Cathy, she rarely ever thought of herself as Emily any more. Emily belonged to San Francisco, which she never wanted to see again. Cathy had been her late father's pet name for her—the middle name she'd been given at birth was Cathleen—and slipping back into it had felt comfortable, natural.

Her bare, tanned legs stretched out in front of her, Cathy leaned back in a chaise longue and scanned the area near the harbor from behind her sunglasses. Two giant cruise ships inched their way across the serene blue water to the docks. Beyond the bustling waterfront the red-roofed buildings of Charlotte Amalie spread out over the green slopes of Denmark Hill, their white walls glistening in the October sun. Higher up the hill sat Government House, its flags dancing in the gentle breeze.

Even though she had lived surrounded by this verdant paradise for five months now, she was continually being surprised by its breathtaking beauty. She loved the Virgin Islands and thought she could be content, living there indefinitely. And she enjoyed her job, working five afternoons a week in an art gallery.

If she managed prudently, her wages, together with the money she'd brought with her from San Francisco, would provide comfortably for her and Angel the next two years. When Angel was five, Cathy could enroll her in an all-day private kindergarten and work full-time at the gallery. But she was always aware that she couldn't allow any place to feel too permanent. Each day could be their last in St. Thomas. She might have to pick up and leave at any time. There was no absolute safety anywhere.

She heard a step behind her and turned her head sharply as Gwen Nettleton, in a brief lime-colored bikini, dropped into a deck chair. Gwen was Cathy's friend and Angel's baby-sitter.

"Didn't mean to startle you," Gwen apologized. She plucked a bottle of suntan oil from her canvas tote and began slathering her already bronzed arms and legs.

"The children asleep?" Gwen's son, Eric, was six, her daughter, Dawn, four.

"Uh-huh. Thank God for naptime. My two should be good for three hours. They're worn out from spending the morning on the beach. I should have my head examined, letting them talk me into going there on Sunday. There was barely room to spread a beach towel." She grimaced and raked thick auburn hair back with scarlet-tipped fingers. "Dawn wanted to gather shells. Did you and Angel get out this morning?"

Cathy was staring at the terrace of the small hotel several hundred yards from the apartment building. "Only as far as the grocery store," she murmured absently.

The man had been looking straight at her when she'd first noticed him. Now he was lying on his stomach on a towel, his head turned toward the apartment building. His face was hidden by his outstretched arm.

"My alimony check came yesterday," Gwen said. "Want to go shopping tomorrow morning? Nicole's is having a sale."

"No, I don't think so. I can't afford to spend anything on clothes right now."

"How did I know you'd say that?" Gwen sighed. Early in their friendship, Cathy had told Gwen that her husband had died unexpectedly a year previously, and that there had been no life insurance and barely enough money in the bank to last a year—two, if Cathy worked part-time.

She routinely turned down Gwen's invitations to go shopping. Even on the rare occasions when she accepted, she only went along to spectate as Gwen swept from shop to shop, trying on clothes for which there was no longer room in her closets.

"Don't you ever forget the budget and just cut loose?"

The man Cathy had noticed could still be peering at her through that little crack between his arm and the towel. She was sure it was the same man she'd noticed yesterday as she returned home from work. He'd been in front of the hotel, just standing there, his hands in his pockets, as though he were waiting for someone. He'd looked intently at Cathy as she walked by and then had turned abruptly, as though he'd forgotten something, and gone back into the hotel.

"Cathy?"

Cathy was trying to quell the frisson of irrational alarm that rose in her throat. "That man, the one in

the brown bathing trunks lying on this side of the hotel pool.''

Gwen squinted against the sun. ''What about him?''

''I think he's watching me—us.''

Gwen grinned. ''Let me explain something to you,
Cathy. It's when men *stop* watching you that you need
to worry.''

''No, I don't mean that.''

''What then?''

What indeed? From the moment she'd seen this man
yesterday, she'd felt watched. But she'd had that feeling often the past year, especially while they were in
Houston. There, she'd been so paranoid that she'd left
the apartment only when necessary.

Once on the way to visit Rachel, she'd become so
convinced she was being followed that she'd fallen into
hysterics when Rachel had opened her office door.
Rachel Ord, a friend from college days as well as her
attorney, had calmed her down with a martini and
sensible straight talk before taking care of business and
then putting Cathy into a taxi.

No one had followed Cathy home. Her ''tail'' had
been a product of her overworked imagination, like all
the other times. The odds were very good that this time
was no different.

''Cathy! Have you lapsed into a coma?''

''Oh. Sorry.''

''You say that guy who looks like a beached whale—
a very sunburned beached whale—wasn't watching you
in the usual way. What do you mean?''

''Don't pay any attention to me. I'm being silly.''

''Do you know him?''

''No.''

"Know what your problem is? You haven't been with a man in so long, you've forgotten what it's about. When *are* you going to give up your widow's weeds and get back into circulation?"

"Widow's weeds?"

"A figure of speech, and you haven't answered my question. When?"

"When I'm ready," said Cathy shortly, rising. "I think I'll make iced tea. Want a glass?"

Gwen lifted a negligent hand. "As long as you're going. But you don't fool me, Cathy. You just don't want to talk about *that* subject. You never do. Mourning is okay, for a while, but you can't make a career of it. It's sick, my dear."

Cathy shrugged noncommittally and went inside. She preferred Gwen to think she was mourning for a dead husband rather than in dread of a living one, which would elicit too many questions she couldn't answer. For example: How could you be married to a man for four years and not know what he was?

When she returned with tall glasses of iced tea, the man who'd been watching her—who she'd *felt* was watching her—was gone. Which proved he hadn't been paying any particular attention to her in the first place, didn't it?

"Your admirer went inside," Gwen said, accepting the tea.

"Yes," Cathy replied with a calm that belied her lingering anxiety.

"He was too old for you, anyway. Nothing to look at, either."

"Gwen—"

"I say you should give Lyle Wenger a chance." Lyle owned Impressions, the gallery where Cathy worked.

An easy, casual friendship had developed between them, but Lyle had made no attempt to take the relationship beyond that. Of course, the past year she hadn't been the least bit interested in becoming involved with anyone, and Lyle was good at reading people. Now that she thought about it, she realized Lyle must be one of Charlotte Amalie's most eligible bachelors.

"Why spoil a nice friendship?" Cathy said. "Good friends are harder to come by than lovers."

Gwen opened her eyes briefly to squint at Cathy. "How would you know?"

"I've learned from watching you," Cathy said, grinning. "Let's see, in the few months I've known you, there's been Peter—" Cathy was counting on her fingers "—Dewey, Stone—I still say *that's* a fictitious name—and I mustn't forget Jeremy. Did I miss anybody?"

Gwen laughed and smoothed back her thick, auburn hair. "No, but I didn't know you were keeping records."

"It's merely friendly interest. I care about you." Cathy spoke lightly, but in truth she cherished the friendship. Apart from Lyle, Gwen was the only friend she'd made lately. Getting too close to people was risky in her situation. Friendships developed over time into a sharing of lives—private thoughts, dark secrets, even pain. Cathy couldn't share that much of herself, though she'd been tempted to unburden herself to Gwen once or twice. She'd always overcome the urge and, always, she'd known she'd made the right decision, the only one.

"Mmm. Well, I think Jeremy may be around for a while. I'm very fond of him. And he likes the kids.

That's a big point in his favor. I never realized until I was divorced how many men can't stand kids. Other people's, anyway."

"Really?"

"Oh, they try to hide it, but it comes out sooner or later." She chuckled. "I'll never forget the time Eric spilled a full glass of grape juice on Peter's yellow linen slacks. It was the first time he'd worn them. The man almost had a nervous breakdown."

"What did you do?"

"Laughed hysterically. I couldn't help it. He threw a temper tantrum worthy of the brattiest three-year-old. Of course, my laughing only made him angrier. He called Eric a grubby, little monster and said I was as ill-mannered as my kids."

"End of romance."

"You'd better believe it. But let's get back to Lyle."

"Let's not," Cathy said firmly.

She couldn't get the man beside the hotel pool out of her mind. She asked herself why. The other men she'd noticed watching her from time to time during the past year had been invariably motivated by the simple interest of a man in a woman he'd like to meet.

She had conjured up far more menacing creatures in the long, still night hours when she couldn't sleep. These men created by her imagination had cold eyes, dead eyes. Like the "business associates" who'd come to see Frank during the years she'd lived on the estate.

Even from the beginning, when she'd still been innocently, naively in love, they had made her feel uneasy. It was nothing they said or did. They were, in fact, flawlessly polite and deferential in her presence. But she had sensed something not quite right about them. It was a long time before she realized it was their eyes. Blue, brown, green, no matter the color, their eyes were as impervious as flint, as though the men had seen too much and were no longer capable of being moved by what they saw. Strangely, Frank's dark eyes had never seemed hard to her until the day she saw through the facade of their marriage to the maze of deceit upon which it was built.

The fiftyish, overweight man beside the hotel pool had appeared to be as far removed from the stereotypical villain as a man could be. In the one brief look she'd had of his eyes, when she'd seen him standing in front of the hotel, she hadn't thought them particularly cold or unfeeling.

Yet there had been interest, and it wasn't sexual; it had been too detached and analytical. She'd seen a sharp flicker in his eyes, as though he might have recognized her. He'd started to glance away from her and then, abruptly, had turned back. That was what bothered her, she supposed. She was sure she'd never seen the man before. Maybe Gwen was right and she no longer recognized mere male attentiveness when she was its object.

No, Gwen was wrong. But if that flicker hadn't been because the man thought her an attractive woman, then what was his interest?

For a good part of Sunday night, these and similar thoughts chased each other about Cathy's mind as she alternated between catnapping and wandering through the dark apartment while Angel slept.

By the time Monday's dawn pearled the sky, she'd gotten around to telling herself that the poor man hadn't been watching her at all. He had only appeared to be looking at her while his thoughts were elsewhere.

Smiling to herself, she mentally rephrased the punch line from an old joke: Everybody has to look somewhere.

With the sunrise, she once more embraced objectivity. She would not keep going over the futile, anxious thoughts that had kept her awake most of the night. She had no information upon which to base such thoughts. But she couldn't just let it go, either. Being *almost* sure she was safe wasn't good enough. So she would find out something about the man—his name, what he was doing in Charlotte Amalie.

She didn't know exactly how she would get the information. She doubted that hotel employees would submit to the questioning of a stranger who had literally walked in off the street. Nevertheless, after breakfast she left Angel with Gwen and went to the hotel, trusting that something would occur to her by the time she arrived in the lobby.

Maybe she could sit in the coffee shop until the man appeared. And then what? If there was a woman with him, Cathy might be able to strike up a conversation with her. If not, she wondered if she'd have the courage to speak to the man. Would he think it was a come-on? Well, that was the least of her worries.

What if she simply asked him point-blank why he'd been watching her? Marvelous, she thought wryly. If his motives were sinister, he certainly wouldn't admit it. If not, he'd likely think her deranged.

The sky was a brilliant blue and the breeze carried the faint, salty scent of the sea. The small section of "downtown" Charlotte Amalie that Cathy could see in the distance was already clogged with tourists from the cruise ships making the rounds of the duty-free shops.

As she reached the hotel, a taxi whipped around her and pulled up beneath the green canopy that stretched from the glass lobby doors to the sidewalk. Startled, Cathy stepped back and off the circular drive. Glancing at the uniformed doorman, she hesitated. No clever method of approaching hotel employees for information had magically occurred to her on the short stroll from the apartment building. She gazed at the hotel's revolving door and considered her next move.

A bellboy came out of the hotel, carrying two large suitcases. He was followed by a balding, heavyset man in an oatmeal colored linen jacket. It was the man who'd kept her awake most of the previous night.

Standing there against a blank brick wall, she felt as exposed as a rabbit sprinting across a newly plowed field. Her heart raced anxiously, but to duck out of sight now would only draw more attention to herself.

The taxi driver opened his trunk and took the bags from the bellboy. The heavyset man seemed preoccupied; he didn't notice her at first. He planted one foot on the floor in front of the taxi's back seat and bent to get in. As he did so, his gaze raked Cathy impersonally, not stopping or even hesitating. He acted as though he'd never seen her before in his life.

The black doorman walked toward the taxi. "You have you a good flight home, Mr. Zenke." He spoke in the lilting patois common among blacks who'd grown up on the island. The man called Zenke was in the taxi now. He leaned his head out the back window to salute the doorman. "Thanks, Delmar."

"We 'spect you back next year, like always," said the doorman.

"Count on it. Save a room overlooking the pool for me, so I can watch the pretty girls."

The bellman laughed merrily. "I be doin' that, Mr. Zenke."

The taxi driver got in and slammed the door. Cathy watched the balding head in the back window grow smaller as the taxi drove away. The passenger did not look back. She realized that her hands were trembling. From pure relief. His name was Zenke and he was obviously a harmless tourist in St. Thomas on vacation, a tourist who liked the island so much he returned every year to the same hotel.

There was no need to pack hurriedly and dash to the airport to take the next flight to somewhere else, no need to try to explain to Angel why they were moving again, why she had to leave her playmates, Eric and Dawn, behind, why they had to use new names. She and Angel were still safe—for the present.

If Cathy could have followed the taxi, seen it take the man called Zenke to an office with no identifying information on the door, an office somehow suspicious in its very ordinariness, she might have had second thoughts. If she could have eavesdropped on the conversation between Zenke and a tall, lean man with deep-set hazel eyes, before Zenke returned to the waiting taxi and continued to the airport, she and Angel would have been on the earliest possible flight out of Charlotte Amalie to almost anywhere.

If she could have seen the hard, calculating narrowing of the tall man's hazel eyes, she might also have realized that even a flight to the other side of the world would not carry them to safety this time. She would have known that, far from being safe, she and Angel were in more imminent danger than at any time since they fled San Francisco a year earlier.

Chapter 2

Zenke seems sure she's the right woman," Brown said, "and he's seen her up close twice."

Darrin Boyle's contact in St. Thomas was young, baby-faced, with the type of fair skin that sunburned easily and peeled but never tanned. He was a little nervous and a great deal excited about having a Washington agent in his office. Like Darrin, Brown had come on board straight from law school. He'd been with the bureau less than two years.

St. Thomas was the sort of hinterland that provided postings for new agents while they learned the ropes. Darrin had spent three years in Wichita before being transferred to Washington. Such rapid ascent to headquarters was rare, and he'd been the envy of most of the younger agents stationed around the country. He knew that, behind his back, they'd called him the director's fair-haired boy. A rumor—one of many that had circulated about him at the time—hinted that he was related to the director's wife.

Upon his arrival in Washington, he'd been summoned to the director's office and told he had exactly one year to prove himself or it was back to Wichita or someplace like it. At that moment, he'd almost wished he *did* have a blood connection to somebody in the director's family. After he came to know the director a little, he'd realized it wouldn't have made the slightest difference.

He'd worked hard and been lucky, and now was fairly well entrenched at the capital. The only criticism in his progress reports related to his stubborn tendency to think for himself and act accordingly without first checking with his superiors.

Darrin asked, "Have you seen the woman?"

Brown flushed, as though he suspected the question carried a criticism, one that Darrin didn't intend. "No. The first I heard of it was yesterday. Before then, we didn't even know Zenke was here. He didn't see fit to check in with us."

"I'm sure no slight was intended."

Brown seemed unconvinced.

"Do you check in with the local boys when you're on vacation?"

Brown visibly relaxed and grinned sheepishly. "No. All I'm interested in is forgetting about the job."

"Exactly. Now, I'm probably going to need your help to get an apartment in the woman's building."

"Oh, right," Brown said earnestly. "Vacant apartments are as scarce as hen's teeth. They keep building new ones, but the demand continues to outrun the supply. However, I have a contact in the local government who can probably help us."

"Good. I'll be at the Fisherman's Reef. I'll wait for your call." Darrin hesitated, wondering how much he could say without insulting Brown's intelligence. "It goes without saying that the fewer people who know who I am and why I'm here, the better."

Brown stiffened a little. "Of course."

"I'm Darrin Boyle, a technical writer who's come to St. Thomas to write a couple of computer books."

"Okay." Brown scribbled on a piece of paper and handed it to Darrin. "My home address and phone number, in case you need to reach me and can't find me here. Is there anything else I can do for you?"

"Not at the moment."

"Then I'll get back to you soon." They shook hands and Brown added, "I'll ask someone to drive you to your hotel."

"No, thanks. I'd like to walk around town for a while. I had my bags sent on from the airport."

Darrin left the office feeling better about his contact than when he'd entered. Brown was young but he seemed competent. And, Darrin thought with a smile, he'll bust his rear proving himself to the big gun from headquarters.

The sun was brilliant. Darrin removed his sport jacket and slung it over one shoulder. He ambled along the steep road leading down Denmark Hill. Within a few minutes he arrived at the waterfront. He strolled along Veterans Drive, with the boat-dotted harbor on his left, shops and other business establishments on his right. Sunburned tourists in brief attire milled from one shop to the next, and he had to step aside frequently to allow a knot of them to pass.

Soon tired of fighting the pedestrian traffic, he found a table at a sidewalk café and ordered an iced drink—a piña colada without the rum. He sipped the drink and gazed at the bustle of activity near the harbor. Boats came and went continually, from small sail boats to luxurious yachts. Nut-brown sailors dealt with rigging or lounged on deck. Overhead a few angel hair wisps of clouds trailed through a blue sky that bowled down to meet a bluer sea.

Darrin hadn't visited the Virgin Islands since a brief trip with a classmate's family on Thanksgiving break during his law school days. That trip couldn't have come at a better time for Darrin. He'd lost his widowed mother the previous summer and hadn't been anticipating spending the holiday with Kent and his wife of less than two months. Kent and Leslie were still in the honeymoon stage and, in spite of Kent's assurances to the contrary, Darrin had felt that he'd be intruding.

The classmate who issued the invitation had been a tall, blond girl named Anna. Bright and pretty but too aggressively eager to nail down a partner for life after law school—in the matrimonial as well as professional sense. To his regret Darrin discovered this only after they reached St. Thomas. When they returned to school, he'd eased out of the relationship as deftly as possible.

There had been several women since. He'd even been engaged once. But at the moment, there was no particular woman in his life. A pity, he thought halfseriously. It seemed a shame not to make use of such a romantic setting.

Darrin had not been mistaken in Brown. The agent phoned him on Tuesday to say that he'd secured an apartment for Darrin in Catherine Prentiss's complex.

The one-bedroom flat was in B-wing, as there were no current or impending vacancies in A-wing, where the Prentiss woman's apartment was located. 112A, to be exact.

Darrin assured him that B-wing would be quite satisfactory. "That was fast," he said. "I'm impressed."

"My government contact owed me a favor," Brown explained. "A very big one fortunately. That complex has a long waiting list."

"Then I'm doubly impressed."

"I did a little quiet checking on Catherine Prentiss, too. She works afternoons at an art gallery on Veterans Drive. It's called Impressions. She has a three-year-old daughter named Annette whom she calls Angel. She claims she's a widow. When she's at work, she leaves the child with a woman who lives in the building."

Darrin felt a prickly stirring of tension, the kind runners must feel just before the shot is fired, signaling the start of a race. Frank and Emily Kampion's daughter, Angela, was three. "Good work. You've been busy."

"It's a change from my regular routine."

Probably the understatement of the year, Darrin thought. "It's good to know you're here if I need you."

"All you have to do is ask."

"Thanks, Brown. I'll probably be calling you for another favor or two as things progress."

"You know where to find me."

The next afternoon, while Catherine Prentiss was at the art gallery, Darrin moved into the apartment. It was small but pleasantly decorated in soft grays and greens. The dining area angled off the living room. There, he set up his computer and small printer on the bleached pine table. He placed a stack of fanfold paper on the floor and fed it into the printer. He took the time to type ten pages of one of the book manuscripts into the computer, replacing Kent's byline with his own, and then printed them out and stacked the pages next to the computer.

Finally he arranged pens, pencils, paper clips and notepads on the table. When he was finished, the space looked like the office of a working writer. He would eat his meals at the glass-topped table in the kitchen alcove, which overlooked the apartment's swimming pool. His apartment's terrace, though postage-stamp size, came equipped with a redwood table and chairs and a charcoal grill.

His luck seemed to be holding. From the kitchen window he could see the back entrance to A-wing where Catherine Prentiss lived with Angel. Angel for Angela? From what he'd seen so far, most residents of the apartment complex used the back entrances to come and go, since they were closer to the curving main thoroughfare leading to the town's business district.

Catherine Prentiss worked until five o'clock at the art gallery. At 5:10, Darrin was stationed in the kitchen with a pair of powerful binoculars in his hands. The photographs of Emily Kampion were spread out on the kitchen table.

Almost at once, he recognized the woman who, from Zenke's description, had to be Catherine Prentiss. She wore a bright yellow wraparound skirt with a scoop-necked white top and white sandals. Her slender arms and legs were suntanned a golden brown. Her shoulder-length hair was a darker brown. The strap of a large bag was slung over her shoulder. She approached the building, coming from the direction of the gallery, with an easy, graceful stride.

Taking a deep breath, he lifted the binoculars to his eyes. He caught her in the lens and sharpened the focus. Her eyes were narrowed against the sun and she could not have seen him, even though she appeared to be looking straight at him. A sea breeze riffled her hair, and she lifted a hand to tuck a lock behind her ear. Then, shading her eyes with her hand, she lifted her face and shook back her hair, like some nature nymph reveling in the beauty of her surroundings.

He could not see her eyes well enough to detect the color. She looked smaller than he'd expected and quite slender. If she was the woman he sought, she was twenty-eight years old. She looked younger. She could have been a college student in St. Thomas on holiday.

He watched her hitch the strap of her purse up on her shoulder and pass between the brick pillars marking the back entrance to the apartment building. Her face was turned in profile now, the nose short and straight, the forehead high and smooth. He glanced at one of the photographs on the table, then back at the woman framed in the binoculars' lens. He had, he realized, been holding his breath, and he released it slowly.

Except for the different hair color, the woman entering A-wing could be the same woman whose photographs were spread over the kitchen table. *Could* be. But he needed to see her close up before he'd feel confident enough to move ahead with the investigation.

The woman disappeared into the building. He returned the binoculars to their case, picked up the photographs and carried them to the big armchair in the living room. Propping his feet on a footstool, he leaned back and studied the photographs for what must have been the hundredth—thousandth—time.

With pinpoint concentration, he ignored his growing excitement that, if not controlled, could make him act precipitantly. He knew he couldn't afford to go off half-cocked. She was too clever, and she would be on the alert for anything suspicious, anything out of the ordinary. She had proved herself to be good at this cloak-and-dagger routine, but so was he.

He cleared his mind and centered it in calm, cool logic. He must plan carefully. He would have one chance at her, and only one.

By Thursday afternoon, Darrin had worked out how he would approach her. As he'd walked down to one of Charlotte Amalie's several sidewalk cafés for lunch, he'd stopped to examine the watercolors being hawked on the sidewalk by the artist, a scruffy, ponytailed man in middle-age. The sun had turned the man's skin the color and texture of tanned cowhide.

"You from the States?" he asked Darrin, grinning to expose a gap where a front tooth was missing.

"Yes, Iowa originally," Darrin replied, naming the state where he'd grown up and where Kent still lived.

"The great heartland, eh? I'm from Nebraska myself." He offered a hand. "Jerome Weatherhead."

"Darrin Boyle. How long have you lived in the Virgin Islands?"

The artist laughed. "Came here to live in a commune back in '71. The commune fell apart in about a year, but I stayed. Worked as a dishwasher, busboy, whatever I could get till a couple years ago. My paintings have been supporting me—in a manner of speaking—since then."

"These are nice."

The artist lowered his voice. "Letcha in on a secret. I consign my best work to a local gallery. Impressions, on Veterans Drive."

Darrin almost laughed aloud. His luck just kept on running, and it was about time. "I think I know it. I might drop in and have a look after lunch."

"Hope you do, chum."

Now, having treated himself to a celebratory meal of grilled salmon, Darrin entered the gallery, gazing around interestedly like a tourist strolling in off the street. The gallery was separated into several rooms. Darrin examined the artwork in the showroom he'd entered from the street, taking his time and forcing himself not to look around for Catherine Prentiss. He didn't see any of Weatherhead's work. After a while, he moved on to the next room.

He felt her presence before he saw her. His senses sharpened to capacity. He could smell the sweetness of a subtle perfume, could even hear the softness of breathing and feel the warmth of another body.

She was there, in the room with him.

"May I help you?"

Taking one last, deep bracing breath, he slowly turned from the oil he'd been studying...and stared directly into dark blue eyes.

They were the deepest shade of blue he'd ever seen. Blue like the sea far below the surface—at such a depth that a diver might become disoriented and lose his way. It would be as dangerous for a man to lose himself in those eyes. It was a damn good thing she was simply a source of information to him. He was, therefore, in no danger of succumbing.

She felt as though she'd suddenly been caught in the beam of a powerful light. His deep-set eyes, she thought, were a most unusual color, fascinating. Hazel with the glitter of gold underneath, as though a lamp had been turned on inside his head. Like a calm-colored screen with an aggressive, complex intelligence actively at work behind it.

Probably a trick of the interior lighting, she told herself—and her tendency to be suspicious of every man she met. His six-foot-plus height and broad shoulders dwarfed her five feet five inches. She tilted her head to one side and he lowered his lashes a bit, masking the golden glint of his eyes.

"I'm browsing," he said. Close up, she was even slimmer than what he'd expected from what he'd viewed through his binoculars. He took in the lightly tanned perfection of her skin, the suggestion of a dimple at one corner of her mouth, the small locket hanging from a fragile gold neck chain, the shining brown hair. If dyed, it was an excellent job. She wore no other jewelry, not even a wedding ring, he noted.

She was dressed simply—fashionably, he supposed, though he was not inclined to pay much attention to women's fashions—in a red cotton knit shirt and matching skirt gathered on an elasticized waistband. On her feet were tan sandals. Her legs were bare.

He'd expected someone married to a multimillionaire to be dressed more expensively. And considering what her husband did for a living, he'd expected someone more showy, brassy even. It was obvious that this woman had class, as obvious as the fact that she had a natural beauty that the most ordinary clothes couldn't hide. He was aware that he resented her beauty and the way she was dressed, though he didn't know why.

"Take your time. We welcome browsers." Her voice was as soft and smooth as combed cotton. "I'll leave you to your own devices."

She turned and walked back toward the showroom from which she'd emerged. Watching the slight, graceful sway of her hips, he had a flicker of doubt. Perhaps she wasn't what he'd expected because she wasn't Emily Kampion. Maybe she was exactly who she said she was.

He took a step to follow her, then forced himself to wait, to stand idly with his hands in the pockets of his walking shorts. "Actually," he said hesitantly, "I didn't come in here by chance." She paused and turned back to him with a questioning expression. "I'm looking for something by a local artist. I saw some of his work this morning on the street. He told me he consigns his best work to this gallery."

"Describe him for me."

"Ponytail, missing front tooth. Sort of an aging hippie type. He said his name was Withers, Weathers, something like that," he said doubtfully, though he remembered the artist's name perfectly well.

"Jerome Weatherhead."

"That's the one."

She chuckled and it was like the sound of water trickling over smooth stones. "Jerome's something of a local character. But he's beginning to get a respectable following—well deserved in my opinion. It's true that Lyle Wenger, the owner of this gallery, gets first choice of everything Jerome does."

"Do you have any of his work at the moment?"

"A few watercolors. Come with me and I'll show you."

He followed her through two small showrooms and into a third at the back of the gallery. Framed paintings and prints were tastefully arranged on white walls. A few small pieces of sculpture were placed on pedestal stands about the rooms. The floors were bare, polymer-coated white pine. The not unpleasant smells of paint and turpentine hung in the air. The gallery was long and narrow, one room leading into the next in a more or less straight line, so that sunlight streamed into all of the rooms through long windows.

She's at home here, he thought. She must enjoy working in the gallery, for if she was Emily Kampion she certainly didn't have to work. He would have thought tying herself down to a job, one which surely must not pay a great deal, would be the last thing she'd want to do. Somehow it raised her a notch in his estimation. And then he wondered why it should. If she was the woman they'd been searching for, the job was a very calculated move. Nobody expected to find Frank Kampion's wife working for wages. It was a perfect cover.

"These are Jerome's." She had stopped in front of four watercolors arranged as a group.

He ambled over to stand beside her and study the paintings. They were scenes of St. Thomas—one of Charlotte Amalie's harbor with Denmark Hill in the background, another of a deserted, windswept beach with a few gulls wheeling over white sand against a pale turquoise sky. The other two were of Charlotte Amalie street scenes, one at midday, the other at night.

"I like these better than what he had for sale on the street," Darrin commented. "The colors are more subdued."

She glanced up at him approvingly. "He splashes paint on canvas for the tourist trade—three or four paintings in one day—and sells them just as quickly because they're inexpensively priced. But when he's being serious, he's more subtle."

"Obviously these weren't dashed off in a few minutes' time."

"No."

There was a door marked Private in the back wall of the showroom. From behind the door came the muted strains of a Mozart sonata. He wondered whose choice the music was—hers or her boss's?

"Lyle isn't here just now," she said, as though she'd read his thoughts, "but I could give you a ten percent discount on any of these."

So, she had chosen the Mozart. Another surprise. She was full of them, it seemed. Although he was looking at the watercolors, he was aware of her shoulder almost touching his arm, a shoulder delicately delineated beneath the cotton knit of her shirt. Aware of the light scent of her perfume. Aware of the incredibly narrow wrist and slender hand that she raised toward one of the paintings. "Notice the gradations of color here along the horizon." Her fingernails were smoothly shaped, gently curved, painted with an unobtrusive clear polish.

"Mmm," he mused, conscious of the dark blue eyes on his face.

"I don't know whether you're interested in art as an investment—"

"Not really." He met her impersonal gaze for a moment and felt the prickly stirrings of anger. Did she have to be so damned good at this role she was playing? For she *was* playing a role. He was as sure as he could be without concrete proof. She had Emily Kampion's eyes. "I don't know enough about it to be an investor."

"But you know what you like," she finished for him with a smile. "Well, I think you could live with a Weatherhead from now on. They wear well. There's also a good possibility that it could turn out to be a smart investment, not that it's guaranteed. One never knows what will strike the art world's fancy ten or twenty years down the line."

"I don't care about that right now. I recently moved into a new place, and I need something to hang on my living room wall." His mouth quirked into a crooked grin. "I'll bet you don't get many people as ignorant of artistic subtleties as I am."

Cathy weighed his admission and thought it sincere. "You'd be surprised."

He turned back to the watercolors. "I like these two." He indicated the harbor and beach views. "What do you think?"

"The beach scene is my favorite," she admitted. "I'd have to toss a coin to choose among the other three. They're all excellent."

"Spoken like a good saleswoman."

A small frown slipped across her face. "I wouldn't dream of talking a customer into buying a work he was uncertain about."

"I was only kidding."

The frown disappeared. "Are you taking the two, then?"

"Yes."

"What about the frames?"

"I'll need them, too."

"I'll wrap these for you." She lifted one of the paintings from the wall, and he got the other. He followed her to the office where the music was playing, and lounged in the doorway while she wrapped the watercolors separately in brown paper and tied them with twine. She took a small hand calculator from a desk drawer and figured the cost. He paid cash, not sure he could write such a large check so soon on the account he'd opened at a local bank the previous day, and she might become suspicious if he wrote one on his Washington bank.

"You said you'd moved recently. Did you move from somewhere else in Charlotte Amalie?" she asked as she unlocked a cash drawer and tucked the bills inside. It sounded as though she were only making conversation, but he suspected she was more interested in his answer than she seemed. She was a woman in hiding, and any stranger she met would be someone to be suspicious of.

"No, I'm new in town."

"Where did you live before?" This time he detected a flicker of wariness in her eyes.

"Most recently Chicago," he replied amiably, plucking the city from the air because he knew it well. "I can do my job anywhere I like, so I've moved around a lot."

"What do you do?"

"I'm a writer. I've signed a new book contract that should keep me busy for eight or nine months, so I expect to be here at least that long."

She watched him closely as he replied, and she seemed to be weighing his answer. Then her eyes warmed, as though she'd decided she could accept his words at face value. She handed him the paintings. "You'll want to unwrap these as soon as possible. I hope you enjoy them."

"I'm sure I will." He wanted to stay longer, to engage her in further conversation, but there was no good excuse for his doing so. They hadn't even introduced themselves. To give his name now might make it obvious that he was reluctant to go, so he simply said, "Thank you," and left.

He didn't see her again until Saturday. He didn't leave the apartment on Friday at all, for fear of running into her by chance and putting her on guard. Two days in a row might appear too obviously contrived.

He typed more of Kent's manuscript into his computer and printed it out. He locked Kent's manuscript away in his attaché case when he wasn't using it. It wouldn't do for anyone to discover that he was working daily on an already completed manuscript. He passed some time going through the fifty pages he'd printed out so far and editing them with a pen. He wasn't the world's best typist, so there were plenty of typos to correct.

Saturday afternoon, when he was in the kitchen getting a soft drink from the refrigerator, he saw Catherine Prentiss leave A-wing with a little girl. They set off walking in the direction of the shopping district.

It would be convenient if he should be walking back from the opposite direction when they returned. Surely nobody could think it anything but a chance meeting. He pulled a kitchen chair away from the table and straddled the seat. His arms folded across the back, he sipped the cola and thought about it.

He'd gone into the gallery on Thursday, two days ago. Was it too soon to arrange another ''chance'' meeting? He had to do it eventually and without wasting much more time, yet he was aware of an odd reluctance to take the next step. Why was that? he wondered.

The thought flitted across his mind that perhaps he was reluctant to use the woman he'd talked to in the art gallery, the woman who called herself Catherine Prentiss. But he banished the thought immediately. He frequently used informants in the course of an investigation, and he'd never felt the slightest hesitation before. Informants—voluntary or otherwise— were a necessity of life in his business. His reluctance, he decided, probably derived from the fact that, as he came to know Catherine Prentiss better, he might discover that she wasn't who he hoped she was, that he'd been wasting his time.

After thinking about it, he told himself that the woman wasn't apt to become any more suspicious if she ran into him again today than if he put off the meeting until next week.

Two hours later, when Cathy and Angel strolled back to the apartment after buying a new book for Angel, Darrin, in shorts and a knit shirt, ambled toward them from the opposite direction. His binoculars dangled from a strap around his neck.

He studiously avoided looking at them, pretending to be interested in some wind surfers in the distance. He managed to barely avoid running into them at the entrance to the apartment complex.

"I'm sorry. Oh, hello." He halted and let his gaze roam the woman's face, as though he were trying to place where he'd seen her before.

"Hello." She smiled uncertainly, but she seemed to be buying his act.

He lifted his shoulders as though in apology. "I know we've met . . . somewhere." He should have been an actor, he told himself. He grinned suddenly, self-deprecatingly. "That's not a line, really." He let the light dawn on his face and snapped his fingers. "I've got it—the art gallery. You sold me two watercolors."

"That's right."

He extended his hand. "I'm Darrin Boyle. I'm sorry I almost ran over you." He touched the binoculars. "I've been down at the harbor watching the ships. I saw a yacht that made my mouth water. I guess I still had my mind on that."

She shook his hand. "Cathy Prentiss. I understand perfectly."

"Are you a yacht enthusiast?" he asked.

"I've never even been on one, but sometimes I think it would be fun to live on a boat. It seems a carefree existence." And so convenient when you had to change addresses in a hurry, she added to herself.

He grinned, thinking that Frank Kampion could buy her ten yachts if she really wanted them. His gaze dropped to the brown-haired child who clung to her mother's hand. "Who's your first mate here?"

"This is my daughter, Angel. Say hello to Mr. Boyle, sweetheart."

"Hi," the child whispered, pressing shyly against her mother's leg.

"Do you live in this complex?" Cathy asked.

"Yeah, in B-wing. You, too?"

"In this wing." She was eyeing him with curiosity now, and some speculation. "I'm surprised you could get in. I understand there's a waiting list."

"True. I've had my name on it since the first of the year." Brown had assured him that the apartment manager would confirm this, if questioned. Darrin hadn't met the manager yet, nor had he any particular need or desire to do so. "My publisher checked into it for me and arranged to get me in line."

The speculation faded from her eyes. "A wait of ten months to a year is pretty standard for the good buildings. Well, nice to see you again. We'd better go in. It's time for Angel's nap."

He said goodbye and walked toward B-wing. He thought he'd pulled it off without arousing her suspicions. He felt a bit smug. Still, he mustn't push his luck. He'd better give her several days to get used to the idea that he lived in the complex before he ran into her again.

It would take some thought, figuring out how to set up another meeting. Eventually he had to get into her apartment and look for evidence that a man was or had been staying there, or was expected in the near future. Where *was* Kampion? He wasn't staying on the estate near San Francisco. Nor had he been spotted anywhere else for the past year.

Cathy. Perversely, the name suited her. What an elaborate masquerade she was playing. Evidently she expected to be in Charlotte Amalie for some time—she'd taken a job. It followed that, if she was Emily, she expected Kampion to join her there. And since she was supposed to be widowed, he wouldn't enter the scene as her husband. Would he pose as her brother? Maybe, or he might pretend to be a new man in her life and go through the motions of courting her.

After a year in hiding, they must be feeling pretty damned safe. It might make them cocky, reckless.

If so, Darrin would be waiting—and ready.

Chapter 3

Moments later, Cathy was putting her daughter down for an afternoon nap. "Night-night, sweetheart."

"You promised we'd go swimming after my nap," Angel murmured with a yawn.

"I remember." Cathy kissed her daughter's brow and closed the venetian blinds, plunging the bedroom in smoky shadows. She left the room, pulling the door shut behind her.

She went into the kitchen, made a glass of iced lemonade and carried it to the living room where she sank into a comfortable armchair. The walk to town and back, with the sun blazing, had wearied her.

Sighing, Cathy rested her head against the chair's high back. The room's slatted blinds were angled so that ribs of bright sunlight striped the ceiling. The only sound was the dim hum of the air conditioning. She sipped the lemonade, feeling her eyelids grow heavy. She felt tired enough to nap herself.

She finished her drink, set the glass aside and settled more comfortably in the chair. Maddeningly, once she'd decided to nap, her eyelids no longer felt heavy. She gazed idly around her.

It was a pleasant room, decorated in tans and blues and rose hues, all three colors being repeated in the hazy southwestern prints she'd chosen for the walls. The furniture, which had come with the apartment, was comfortably padded and upholstered in nubby rose and blue fabrics. The morning newspaper lay folded at the end of the couch on the tan-carpeted floor. Several green plants in straw containers, which Cathy had added, gave the room a homey touch.

In addition to the large living room, the apartment contained dining room, kitchen, two good-sized bedrooms and two baths. Cathy and Angel had lived there for three months. Cathy had felt more at home there than in any of the other places they'd lived since that dreadful, panicked flight from San Francisco to Houston a year ago.

She had put her name on the waiting list as soon as they came to Charlotte Amalie. Having picked the address from a phone book, she arrived in the building manager's office, exhausted and bedraggled, directly from the airport, with a whining Angel in tow.

The manager had put her name on the list and even called around to find a small three-room furnished flat for them to move into while they waited. Since it was old, not well maintained, and in an undesirable location, it hadn't rented the second it hit the market. She had found the place depressing, but there had been nowhere else to go.

She must have been a pathetic sight, walking into the manager's office, carrying two big suitcases and with a tired and cranky Angel hanging on to her skirt. Evidently he'd felt sorry for her and moved her name to the top of his list, for he'd called two months later to say he had an opening.

It hadn't occurred to her at the time that she'd received preferential treatment. But after moving in, she'd learned from other tenants that a year's wait for a place in the complex wasn't uncommon.

Darrin Boyle had waited ten months. Odd that she'd never laid eyes on many of the residents in the sprawling complex, but already she'd run into Darrin Boyle twice, and he'd only recently moved in.

Maybe it wasn't so odd, after all. It was entirely possible, she thought with consternation, that she was simply more aware of him than of other tenants. If she was preoccupied, as was often the case, she could pass a neighbor on the grounds without even seeing him.

Even though getting involved with a man was the farthest thing from Cathy's mind, she couldn't help noticing that Darrin Boyle was attractive. Tall and broad-shouldered with a lean, intelligent face. Light brown hair and brows, straight nose, strong chin with a faint cleft. But it was his gold-flecked, hazel eyes that you noticed first, the way they lit up, as with an inner flame, when his attention was engaged. All in all, he had the physical attributes producers must look for when casting the lead for a romantic adventure film. He definitely had what her college drama teacher would have called magnetism.

A very attractive man. She might not be in the market, but neither was she blind.

No one could be further removed from the hood types she expected Frank to have hired to search for her. She took comfort in that thought for a few moments, until she remembered how cunning Frank was, cunning enough for her to have swallowed his monstrous lies without question for four years. Even Rachel had found that hard to believe, and Rachel was an old friend.

"But didn't you wonder why he had all those armed guards around?" Rachel had asked that first evening, after she and Angel had landed on Rachel's doorstep in Houston. When Angel was asleep, she had told Rachel everything.

"He said they were there to protect the art collection," she had replied defensively. "He owns a van Gogh, two Renoirs and dozens of other valuable paintings by lesser known artists."

"Good God," Rachel had said, wide-eyed, and then added grimly, "I guess blood money spends as easily as any other kind."

"After I found out and . . . and told him I wanted a divorce, I was never again allowed to take Angel off the estate unless a guard accompanied us. If one of the maids hadn't helped me, I couldn't have gotten her away."

Cathy shuddered, remembering that night and the many that followed, when she had been sure every stranger who looked at her on the street, every sound in the night, every ring of the doorbell was somebody sent by Frank to take her and Angel back.

Sometimes she could hardly believe that she'd eluded them for a year. Sometimes she thought it was a dream from which she would wake any second and find herself back on the estate with the high fence and the guards and the dogs.

Because Frank was highly intelligent and crafty, a dangerous combination. He was crafty enough to send a man after her who looked like anything but a hired gun. Somebody like Darrin Boyle?

Maybe she should check him out to be sure, find out if he really was a writer, as he said.

Stop it, she told herself wearily, just stop it. Darrin Boyle couldn't have moved into an apartment in the complex unless he'd been on the waiting list for ten months, as he claimed. And ten months ago, she'd been in Houston. Then, even she hadn't known that, months later, she would be living in Charlotte Amalie, much less in this particular apartment building.

Frank's hirelings wouldn't rent an apartment, anyway. If they ever found Cathy and Angel, they'd waste no time forcing them on a plane bound for California. Or perhaps they'd only take Angel and leave Cathy behind, which would be even worse. Furthermore, somebody employed by Frank wouldn't call attention to himself by coming into the gallery and stopping to talk to her on the street, as Boyle had done.

After thinking it through logically, Cathy felt reassured. She was even able to nap for a short while.

She didn't see Darrin again until several days later. She and Gwen had taken their three children to a nearby hamburger restaurant for dinner. Afterward, Angel, Eric and Dawn were playing hide-and-seek in Gwen's apartment, while Gwen and Cathy chatted on the terrace.

It was dusk and, down near the harbor, the lights of Charlotte Amalie were beginning to blink on, one by one. Gwen had just reminded the children for about the tenth time not to run in the apartment, when Darrin, shirtless and wearing running shorts and shoes, jogged by on the narrow bike path that wound through the grounds of the complex. He waved and called hello, but kept on running.

Cathy was surprised when Gwen called back, "Looking good, Darrin!"

"Darrin?" Cathy said with a wry grin. "Mr. Boyle does get around, doesn't he?"

"You've met him, too?" Gwen asked.

"He bought a couple of watercolors at the gallery. I understand he lives in B-wing."

"In 105B. He signed a six-month lease."

Cathy laughed. "You've got it all right on the tip of your tongue. I suppose you've already been invited over for a drink."

"No," Gwen responded somewhat ruefully. "I met him in the laundry room the other day and we got to talking. There's time for a lengthy conversation when you're waiting for your clothes to be washed and dried."

"So what else did you learn about him?"

"He's a writer. He has a contract for two books."

"I already knew that."

Gwen cocked an eyebrow. "It sounds as though you had a rather lengthy conversation with Darrin yourself."

"Not at all. He mentioned that he was a writer while I was wrapping his watercolors. He bought two of Jerome Weatherhead's."

"Hmm. Not only is he a very nice man, but he has good taste." Gwen was one of Jerome Weatherhead's local boosters. She had two of his oils and never lost an opportunity to send people to the gallery to buy a Weatherhead "before he really catches on and the prices go through the ceiling."

"He doesn't know anything about art."

"Well, then, why don't you teach him?"

"Let him take a course."

Gwen chuckled at the clipped rejoinder and wisely allowed the subject to drop.

Cathy recalled the conversation later, after she and Angel returned to their apartment. What Darrin Boyle had told Gwen jibed exactly with what he'd told Cathy. It was one more comforting scrap of data to add to the others she'd collected. There was no underlying sinister motive for his sudden appearance in Charlotte Amalie. Therefore, she needn't be afraid of him.

So why was she so *aware* of him? Why did she feel that little jolt of energy every time his piercing gaze connected with hers?

Whatever the reason, it had nothing to do with Frank or his henchmen. Still, there was something in Darrin Boyle's intense eyes that issued a challenge. Something that she might have labeled sensual, had she allowed herself to dwell on it. She realized that she found Darrin Boyle a bit scary. Beyond that, she did not wish to examine the question.

"I thought you'd been abducted." Rainey's raspy voice exploded from the telephone receiver the instant Darrin picked it up, even before he'd finished saying hello.

"Don't pay the ransom demand," Darrin shot back. "You know it encourages terrorism." He'd been about to get a cold drink from the refrigerator when the telephone rang. Now he stretched the coiled line on the kitchen wall phone to its limit in order to reach the refrigerator door and open it. He surveyed the canned drinks on the bottom shelf, selecting a cream soda and flipped the tab.

"Very funny. It's been nearly two weeks. I had to contact Brown to find out where you were. Damn it, Boyle, I told you—"

"Why run up my expense account with long-distance calls when there's nothing to report? Tsk, tsk, are you suggesting I squander the taxpayers' money?" Soda in one hand, phone receiver in the other, he hooked a chair with his foot and dragged it away from the table. He straddled it backward and leaned one forearm on its back.

"You moved into the woman's building! That's something to report."

"I don't work well with people looking over my shoulder," Darrin said, chagrin sharpening his tone. "You know that."

"And I look incompetent when I have to go to the weekly briefing and say you haven't checked in since you left town." Without replying, Darrin took a long swallow of cream soda. After a few moments Rainey added in a faintly conciliatory tone, "Okay, so I lied. I said you'd reported in a couple of times and you were still trying to confirm the woman's identity."

"That about sums it up."

"Have you even met her yet?"

"Yes, and as far as I can tell she believes I'm who I say I am. I don't want to press my luck and make her suspicious. She'll fly the coop and we could be another year finding her again."

"It's to your advantage to make sure that doesn't happen," Rainey groused. "Trust me."

"That's what I'm trying to do. Look, I think she's our woman. I'm as sure as I can be without concrete proof."

"Then get the proof."

"I'm working on it," Darrin said with deliberate blandness. If Rainey thought he could do the job better, let him take over. With Rainey's legendary impatience, he'd screw things up the first day.

"You haven't seen anybody who could be The Man anywhere around?"

"Nope." Catching a glimpse of movement at the back exit of A-wing, Darrin set down the cola and grabbed the binoculars. Cathy Prentiss, in white shorts and shirt, and Angel, wearing her bathing suit, were leaving the building. Cathy carried a large canvas bag. Apparently they were heading for the apartment pool or the beach. "She has a young child with her, though."

"A child!" Rainey sputtered. "The child is with her and you didn't think it worth reporting! Good God, what does it take to merit a phone call?"

"A driver's license with a certain name on it. A letter addressed to Catherine Prentiss from Frank Kampion, preferably with a current return address."

Rainey sighed heavily. "When can I expect to hear from you?"

Darrin watched as the woman and child bypassed the pool and disappeared beyond the building. The destination was the beach, then. "When I have something substantial to report. Cut me some slack, Rainey."

The other man's oath was swallowed by a hacking cough. When he could speak, he complained, "That's what I've been doing since the day I met you."

"And don't think I don't appreciate it," Darrin said. "I'm going to hang up now. Don't call me, old man, I'll call you." He disconnected in the middle of another cough.

Darrin strode into the bedroom, lifted a stack of underwear in the top dresser drawer and extracted a key ring. The ring contained several odd-looking tools, which would have been recognized immediately as lock-picks by a burglar.

Cathy and Angel should be absent from their apartment for at least an hour. Darrin was aware that he could have entered the apartment any afternoon the past week while Cathy was at work and Angel was down the hall with Gwen Nettleton. He probably would have had more time to look around. What had stopped him was the knowledge that Gwen had a key to the apartment and occasionally let herself in to get a toy or item of clothing that Angel wanted. He'd run into her Monday as she was leaving her apartment, and she'd said she had to get Angel a change of clothes from Cathy's apartment. When Gwen wasn't looking, Angel and Gwen's daughter, fully clothed, had dragged a chair into the shower and turned on the water.

But Gwen would have no reason to use her key on Saturday while Angel was with her mother.

Entering A-wing, he ambled silently down the carpeted hall, hands stuffed in the pockets of his walking shorts, prepared to stroll on out the opposite end of the curving wing if he met anyone. But the wing was quiet, and he saw no one.

When he reached the Prentiss apartment, he glanced both ways before stepping to the door. After a few seconds' silent work with the picks, he stepped inside and quickly closed the door behind him.

He was enclosed by a dim coolness and the particular hush that only unoccupied residences have. There was a faint scent of feminine perfume in the living room and, as he neared the kitchen, the cinnamony smell of recently baked cookies that were cooling on a plate near the stove. He rarely got home-cooking and was sorely tempted to help himself to a couple of cookies, but he overcame the temptation. The cookies might be missed.

He walked quickly through all the rooms, making sure the draperies and blinds were closed before he switched on lights. Cathy Prentiss was a good housekeeper. The kitchen and bathroom tiles sparkled and tabletops gleamed. There was no clutter except in Angel's bedroom, where a few toys and books were scattered about. He conducted a thorough search, leaving everything exactly as he'd found it.

In less than a half hour, Darrin had searched all the closets and drawers in the apartment, as well as beneath mattresses, inside the lining of the draperies, and every other nook and cranny that could be used as a hiding place. He found no evidence that a man had ever occupied, or even visited, the apartment. There was no identification of any sort, either, except for an electric bill addressed to Catherine Prentiss in a kitchen drawer. No personal letters or address book, no driver's license, no credit cards. Nothing. If Cathy possessed any of these in either the name of Catherine Prentiss or of Emily Kampion, she had taken it with her.

Finally, Darrin looked through the kitchen cabinets, lifting the glasses and dishes, one by one, and meticulously replacing them, in case anything was hidden beneath them. In a dark corner of a top shelf, his fingers closed around a small bottle. He pulled it forward to read the label: Naturally Beautiful and below the words Medium Brown. The price stamped on the label was $25.95. Hair dye. Very good dye judging from the price and from the perfectly natural appearance of Cathy's and Angel's hair.

He set the bottle back in the cabinet corner, thinking that it was strong evidence that Cathy Prentiss colored her hair, but beyond that it proved nothing. Many women colored their hair. That didn't mean they were all using false identities. He avoided delving too closely into his reluctance to leap to that conclusion in this particular case. Instead, he imagined how easily a good defense lawyer could dispense with a bottle of hair dye as evidence in a courtroom.

He walked back through the rooms, making a last check to assure himself that everything was as he'd found it, then let himself quietly out of the apartment.

Returning to the apartment an hour later, Cathy sensed a foreign essence the second she followed Angel inside.

"I want milk and cookies," Angel demanded. She was hot and cross after the outing. Despite the sunblock lotion Cathy had bathed her in, Angel's pert little nose was sunburned.

Cathy grabbed the child's hands as she started for the kitchen. "Wait a minute, sweetheart." She scanned the living room quickly and noticed nothing amiss, yet she couldn't shake the feeling that they weren't alone. "Wait right here by the door a minute while Mommy looks around."

"I'm hungry," Angel whined.

"Do as I say, Angel," Cathy said and reached for the brass letter opener lying on the walnut secretary near the front door.

Angel sniffled irritably, but she did as she was told, knowing by her mother's tone that she meant business. Cathy went through the apartment, gripping the letter opener in front of her, aware even as she looked into closets and under beds that she made a ridiculous picture.

Nobody was there, and as far as Cathy could tell, nothing in the apartment had been disturbed. She let the hand grasping the letter opener drop to her side and returned to the living room. Get a grip on yourself, she lectured silently. You'll make Angel a nervous wreck if you don't. It was necessary to remain cautious and alert, but she had to create a normal life for Angel, too. There was nothing normal about a mother who jumped at shadows.

She peeled off Angel's bathing suit and dressed her in a cool sundress before settling her at the kitchen table with a glass of milk and a cookie. With Angel content for the moment, she removed her own still-damp suit, which she wore under her clothes. After dressing again, she hung both suits to dry on a bathroom towel rack.

Had someone been in the apartment while they were out? a small voice persisted. Suppose for a moment that someone had been. Who? If it was someone sent by Frank, her thoughts ran on, he'd have waited for them to return. Unless he preferred to abduct Angel from a place where there was less likelihood of a struggle being overheard. She had a mental picture of Angel being torn from her arms, kicking and weeping. Cathy closed her eyes and shuddered.

A full year had passed. Perhaps Frank had called off the search. In her heart of hearts, she didn't believe he would ever give up. He had warned her if she left him, she'd never see Angel again. He was passionately possessive about what was his, whether it was a Renoir or a daughter.

On the other hand, as events had revealed, she had never really known her husband, so maybe she was wrong in believing he would never rest until Angel was back on the estate and under guard again.

Before returning to the kitchen, she checked the windows and doors in the apartment and found them all locked. As she rejoined Angel, it suddenly occurred to her that Gwen could have let herself into the apartment while they were gone. She couldn't imagine why Gwen would do so when Angel was with Cathy, but she dialed her friend's number anyway. There was no answer.

Sunday afternoon, when Gwen finally answered her telephone, she sounded breathless. Cathy could hear Eric and Dawn arguing in the background.

"I've been trying to reach you all weekend," Cathy said.

"We just walked through the door," Gwen panted. "We spent the weekend in St. Croix with Jeremy." Jeremy Teller, the current man in Gwen's life, owned a hotel in St. Thomas and was considering buying one in St. Croix.

"Oh."

"Eric, stop hitting your sister. Cathy, I'll tell you all about it later. Right now I have to deal with my son."

Pensively, Cathy replaced the receiver. Gwen had been in St. Croix yesterday afternoon, so she couldn't have been in the apartment while Cathy and Angel were at the beach. Nobody, in fact, had been in the apartment, she told herself. Now, forget it.

Angel was having a tea party for her dolls on the terrace. The tea table was a cardboard box with a dish towel spread on top. The tea was apple juice. Watching her daughter fill three tiny cups from a tiny teapot and break off a piece of cookie for each of the tiny plates, Cathy felt her heart swell with love. She would go anywhere, do anything to keep her daughter away from Frank's influence.

Cathy went out and perched on the low rock wall edging the terrace. "Would you like some tea, Mommy?"

"That would be lovely," Cathy said.

Frowning in concentration, Angel filled another of the little cups without spilling a drop and handed it to Cathy. "Thank you, Angel," Cathy said solemnly.

"I'm not Angel. I'm Mrs. Smith and these are my two little girls, Mary and Sally."

"Well, I'm pleased to meet you, Mrs. Smith. You certainly have two well-behaved daughters."

"I know." Angel set the teapot down. Gazing past Cathy's shoulder, she grinned suddenly. "Hi, Darrin! Look, Mommy, it's Darrin." Earlier Angel had reported that one afternoon the previous week Darrin Boyle had shown her and Dawn how to make paper airplanes on Gwen's terrace while Gwen looked on. Apparently, the man had made a conquest of her daughter.

Turning, Cathy saw Darrin Boyle walking toward them. He wore light blue trousers and a white knit shirt. Although he'd only been on the island two weeks, he was already lightly suntanned. Clearly he spent a lot of time outdoors. When did he write? At night?

"Hi," Darrin said, watching as Cathy rose from the rock wall. He smiled, exposing teeth that looked incredibly white in his tanned face. "Having a party, I see."

"Yes." She moistened dry lips. "It's dreadfully hot today, isn't it?"

"Would you like some tea, Darrin?" Angel asked. "It's really apple juice. I'm playing like it's tea."

"Mr. Boyle," Cathy corrected.

"I told her she could call me Darrin," he said. "And I'd love a cup of tea." He took the tiny cup from Angel, holding it between thumb and forefinger. The child's toy looked ridiculous in his big hand.

Cathy kept her eyes on him. He drank from the cup and winked at Angel. "How's the writing going?" she asked.

"Pretty well." Cathy's gaze followed his hand as he handed his cup back to Angel. "I've been getting up at six so I can finish my daily stint before noon. It's hard to stay glued to the computer when I look out my window and see all this." He made a sweeping gesture that included the green grounds behind the apartment building, the sliver of Veterans Drive that could be seen from the terrace, and the harbor beyond.

When he returned his gaze to her face, she averted her eyes, pretending to study the scene he had indicated. "Are you enjoying your watercolors?"

"Yes. But they're still propped up on the living room couch. I can't decide where I should hang them. I don't suppose you would— Look, could you possibly come to my apartment and advise me?"

"Oh." Hastily, she looked back up to meet his eyes. "I, well, if you want me to."

"Are you free right now?"

Refusal was on the tip of her tongue. She didn't know why, only that she didn't want to go to his apartment. Silly, but it seemed an intimate thing to do, even on such a mundane mission. Even as she cast around for a reasonable excuse, he said, "I can't offer you a tea party, but how about a cola or a beer?"

"Can I come?" Angel asked.

Darrin tousled her hair. "I hope so. I need your advice, too. And I have something I found on the beach yesterday I want to give you."

Her tea party forgotten, Angel grabbed Cathy's hand. "Oh, please, Mommy. Can we go?"

Poor little girl, Cathy thought with a pang of guilt. She's so hungry for a man's attention. It took so little to please her.

As for Darrin, he'd asked nothing but her advice on where to hang his watercolors, and she was reacting as though he'd made a pass at her.

"Sure, why not."

His grin flashed, and he swung Angel up to sit on his shoulders. She squealed with delight. "Hang on tight," he said, "and we'll race your mother to the door."

Laughing, Angel grabbed his neck and he trotted off. Cathy followed at a slower pace, thinking that it had been too long since she'd heard Angel laugh with such lack of restraint.

Chapter 4

Excuse the mess," Darrin said, indicating the folders, computer printouts and empty coffee cups strewn over the dining table. On one end of the table, a small computer and dot matrix printer sat side by side. He stacked three cups and picked them up. "I can't work and be neat at the same time." He shrugged good-naturedly. "To be honest, my housekeeping is of the let-things-go-till-you-can't-wade-through-it variety. Fortunately, I could sit down and work in the middle of a junkyard."

Cathy glanced around curiously. The apartment was smaller than hers, one of the single-bedroom units. It was cluttered—books and magazines seemed to have been dropped wherever he finished with them—but it wasn't dirty. The dining area was the only available space large enough to be converted into an office. There was probably a table in the kitchen for meals.

The walls in the living-dining area were completely bare. The two watercolors he'd purchased were propped against the back of the gray couch.

"Let me get rid of these cups," he said, "then you can tell me where I should hang the watercolors."

"You said you have something for me," Angel reminded him.

He grinned. "So I did."

"Where is it?"

"In the kitchen. Come and I'll show you." He went through a swinging door at one end of the living room. Angel trotted at his heels.

Cathy started to call her back, then closed her lips over the words. Angel would argue, and how would she explain her irrational reluctance to let Angel out of her sight while they were in Darrin Boyle's apartment? As long as she could hear their voices, there was nothing to worry about.

Determinedly, she turned to the watercolors. The obvious place for them was over the couch. A couple of throw pillows for the couch in turquoise and white to pick up the colors in the paintings would be nice, but she wasn't about to suggest it. She had no intention of becoming Darrin Boyle's interior decorator. She merely wanted to deal with the paintings and get out of his apartment.

However, as long as she was there, she'd look around to see if anything struck her as suspicious. She *wasn't* being paranoid, she told herself, simply careful. She could still hear Darrin's and Angel's voices coming from the kitchen, and quickly leafed through a couple of the books lying on the coffee table. One was entitled *Introduction to MS-DOS*, the other *Guide to Word*

Processing Software. An interest in computers was hardly a suspicious trait.

She returned the books to the table and was trying to decide whether to chance looking through the papers on the dining room table when Angel burst through the kitchen door without warning, a large seashell held to her ear.

"Look, Mommy. It's a seashell. The ocean's louder than in any of my shells at home."

"That's because it's so big," Cathy said, glad that she hadn't succumbed to the temptation to riffle through Darrin's papers. He had followed Angel into the room and Cathy glanced up to meet his eyes. "Where did you find it?"

"A little cove on the other side of the island. I rented a car one day last week and spent the afternoon driving on back roads."

"It must have just been washed ashore, or some tourist would have latched on to it."

"Probably, although it didn't seem the sort of place that would attract tourists. There were no shops or restaurants nearby. Only a handful of weathered houses up on a little hill. I swam and then wandered along the beach for over an hour and saw no one. It was very peaceful."

Inexplicably, a mental picture flashed into her mind, a picture of him wading out of the ocean to stand alone on a deserted beach, water beading on his broad, tanned shoulders and chest and long, muscled legs.

An odd longing washed over her and she was more aware of the emptiness inside her than she had been at any time since her marriage had crumbled around her. The past year, her mind had been filled with fear that was at times paralyzing, her heart so focused on protecting and keeping Angel with her that there had been nothing left to recognize her needs as a woman. Until this moment, as her gaze melded with his and she couldn't look away. And all the while, his eyes studied her with a stark intensity.

He's the kind of man who would love a woman with everything that's in him, she thought. Was there a woman somewhere whom he loved like that? Strangely, inexplicably, she was saddened by the thought.

I give you my heart and everything else I possess. Frank had said that to her the night he proposed, a lifetime ago. *I will do anything to make you happy.* Lies, all lies. This man was different. She could not imagine those golden eyes lying.

"I'd put the watercolors over the couch," she said, pushing these baffling thoughts and feelings aside.

He stared at her for another instant, as though he found it difficult to look away. But then he walked to the couch and picked up the paintings, saying in the most casual way, "I never know how high to hang pictures. I'll hold them up and you can make a mark when I've got them positioned right. There's a pencil on the table."

Cathy found a pencil and, when she turned around, he was kneeling on the couch, each hand holding a watercolor against the wall. Angel was curled in a chair, her head resting on its upholstered arm, the shell held against her ear.

"A little higher," Cathy said. "No, not that much. There. That looks about right to me."

"I'll take your word for it."

She walked to the couch and, leaning forward, penciled a small dot at the top edge of one of the frames.

"I'd center them above the couch and leave ten or twelve inches of wall space between them."

As she straightened up, her hand struck his shoulder. "I'm sorry," she said, pulling her hand away as though she'd placed it too close to fire. He turned his head toward her and she felt heat creeping up her neck. An odd sort of smile twisted the corner of his mouth, and she moved away from the couch hastily. By the time he'd laid the watercolors on the couch and stood, she had her back to him and she was intently examining a spot on the front of her shirt.

He cleared his throat. "I think somebody's about to fall asleep."

Angel lifted her head from the arm of the chair, protesting, "No, I'm not. I'm waiting for my ice cream bar."

He chuckled. "If it's all right with your mother."

Cathy crossed her arms and turned to face him, running her hands over her upper arms, for there seemed to be a sudden chill in the room. She had recovered from her embarrassment—or whatever it was that had made her feel so flushed as she'd reached over his kneeling form to mark the spot where the watercolors should hang. She forced her thoughts back to practical concerns. "It's all right with me."

"Would you like one?"

"No, thanks." Still, he made no move to go to the kitchen. He merely stood there, studying her in that deliberate way he had. He made her feel her deepest thoughts were exposed to him. It seemed to her that he'd been doing it ever since she'd entered the apartment. She forced her eyes to meet his without wavering. "What's your novel about?"

"I didn't say I was writing a novel."

"You said . . . a book. Two, in fact."

"Books, yes. Computer books aimed at computer-illiterate executives. I write business and technical books."

"Oh." That explained why he'd been reading computer books by other authors. He probably used them as reference sources. "That sounds complicated. How many computer books have you written?"

"Only one, before the one I'm working on now. It was really a manual to be used with word processing software."

"Have you written books on other subjects?"

"Yes. I'll write almost anything I can get paid to write," he said. "I've done several on management techniques and two on how businesses can protect themselves against industrial espionage."

"Espionage. That sounds intriguing."

"The kind Ludlum writes about, yes. The industrial variety is considerably less colorful. It's mostly a matter of copying files." He turned to the child, who was perched on the edge of the armchair, clearly impatient for the treat he'd promised. "What're you waiting for, big'n? Come and tell me which kind of ice cream bar you like. I have three kinds." Over his shoulder, he asked, "Can I get you something to drink, Cathy? Beer? Soft drink? Coffee?"

"I'd like a cup of coffee, if it's not too much trouble," she replied, thinking that he'd probably have to make it, which would give her a few minutes to peek at the papers on his desk.

She moved quickly to the dining room table and leafed through the papers in the folders. They all seemed to contain parts of his computer book manuscript, printed on the dot matrix printer. One folder was entitled Setting Up Your Computer. Another, Getting Comfortable With Your System Unit and Keyboard. Evidently he kept drafts of each chapter in separate folders.

Lying beside the printer were twenty or so pages on fanfold paper. Corrections and additions had been made in ink. The title at the top of the first page was Troubleshooting.

Exactly what you'd expect to find on the desk of a man who was writing a computer book for executives. Afraid to snoop any longer, she moved back into the living room seconds before Darrin pushed open the swinging door and said, "How do you take your coffee?"

She started involuntarily. "Black." The door swung shut again. She took a deep breath and went into the kitchen. Darrin was setting two mugs on the glass-topped kitchen table.

Angel was at the other end of the kitchen, looking out a window through a pair of binoculars, the same binoculars Darrin had had with him the day they ran into him coming back from the harbor. Angel turned when she heard Cathy. She had a mustache of dried chocolate ice cream that made Cathy smile indulgently. "You can see the boats in the harbor and everything, Mommy."

"That's nice," Cathy said distractedly because Darrin had pulled out a chair at the table for her and there was nothing to do but take it.

He sat down opposite her as she lifted her mug in both hands. His long fingers curled around his mug, but he didn't raise it to his mouth. She stared at his fingers for an instant. What would they feel like on her skin, tangled in her hair? She shuddered inwardly, as though waking suddenly, and said, "I think you've made a conquest." She nodded toward Angel, who was once more engrossed in the scene from the kitchen window.

"Where's her father?" he asked quietly, his eyes fixed on her face.

She averted his gaze. It was an obvious question, under the circumstances. "He died . . . a year ago."

He said nothing for so long, she thought he wasn't going to respond. After a while, he said, "It must've been rough on both of you."

She looked at him sharply. There had been a strange edge to his words. Sarcasm? No, of course not. It was just that every nerve in her body tensed when she was asked about her husband, and she sensed connotations that weren't there. "Yes. Angel doesn't ask about him anymore. She was so young when we . . . when we lost him. I don't think she remembers him."

"Tell me about him."

She frowned. He had said the words softly, tonelessly, and the warmth in his eyes had retreated, as though shades had been lowered. It sounded as though he were reading from a script. This was what you said to grieving widows. She resented it. She would have resented it, even if she were truly grieving for a dead husband. Darrin Boyle didn't know her well enough to say those words. She wanted to grab Angel and leave the apartment without a word. She couldn't talk to him about Frank. She didn't even want to think about Frank. And she wasn't going to make up some fairy tale for Darrin Boyle's benefit.

She darted a look across the room at Angel, who was still absorbed in the binoculars. She set her mug down carefully. "I don't have time to drink this, after all. I have some things to do in my apartment.'' She pushed back her chair and stood. ''Thank you, anyway. Angel, we have to go.''

Angel set the binoculars on the window ledge reluctantly. ''I want to get my shell.'' She ran out of the room.

''We'll leave by the back way.'' Cathy went to the door that opened from the kitchen onto the terrace. She was aware that he had come around the table and was standing very close behind her. She could feel his warm breath in her hair, and a nervous chill shivered down her spine.

''I didn't mean to upset you by asking about your husband.'' His voice was low, gravelly.

She took a deep breath and turned to face him. ''I don't like to talk about it in front of Angel. Even when she doesn't seem to be listening, she might be.'' He was too close to her, and her heart skipped a beat. His eyelashes were long and light at the ends as though sunbleached. His eyes were narrowed and brooding. There was a nearly invisible scar above his upper lip.

He stared at her slightly parted lips, as though transfixed. Her mouth would be soft, lush, kissable. Not that her mouth had anything to do with him and his reason for being there. It was simply an idle observation. And as long as he was idly observing, he might as well make note of those incredible, dark blue eyes. They made him think of a tropical sky on a clear night, just before full darkness fell. At the moment they looked naked somehow, utterly vulnerable.

For a split second, an unexpected tenderness washed through him and he wanted to protect her. He lifted his hand and smoothed back a lock of hair that clung to her cheek and heard her sharp intake of breath, felt her flinch. Wonder how long it's been since she was with her husband? he mused.

He frowned. What in hell business was it of his how long it had been? He gathered his wits and stepped back as Angel returned to the kitchen with her seashell. She stopped short and glanced from Darrin to her mother with a questioning look on her face, evidently sensing the tension in the room.

"Ready, sweetheart?" Cathy asked with a brightness that was clearly as false as a counterfeit bill. She turned and fumbled for the doorknob, thankful that, at least, he was no longer touching her. But she could still feel the imprint of his fingers.

"Thank you for the ice cream and the seashell, Darrin," Angel said behind her.

"You bet, big'n. Any time you have a hankering for ice cream, my freezer's always well supplied."

Cathy opened the door and walked out, trusting that Angel would follow quickly. Angel did. Cathy didn't look back as she hurried across a green circle of lawn bordered by beds of drooping white angel's-trumpets, red anthurium and yellow hibiscus. She knew that his eyes followed her. She could feel them.

She can lie like a pro, Darrin thought grimly as he watched the woman and child enter A-wing. *He died...a year ago.* She'd delivered the words with just the right degree of underlying sadness and looked at him with those big, dark, vulnerable eyes. Damn, she was good.

Crazily, there had been a moment when he'd almost believed her, actually wanted to believe her. For an instant, he'd nearly convinced himself that he and Zenke were wrong, that she really was Catherine Prentiss, a widow with a daughter whose name on her birth certificate was Annette Prentiss.

His thoughts puzzled and angered him. He told himself that his momentary urge to protect her was nothing more than a part of his job. Stay close to Frank Kampion's wife and he'd get Kampion eventually. Inevitably there would come a time when the man would have to see his wife and daughter, despite the potential risk involved.

Darrin ignored the possibility that the tender feelings that had assaulted him briefly as Cathy was leaving were more than a dedication to solving the case. He ignored the possibility that maybe, just maybe, this woman with night-blue eyes had gotten to him on some personal level.

He thought about the flush that had stung her cheeks when she'd accidentally touched him, her sharp intake of breath when he'd brushed his fingers across her face. She'd acted like a woman who found him sexually attractive, and he didn't think *that* had been feigned. It must have been a long time since she'd been with her husband. It was possible she hadn't seen him since the three of them disappeared from Kampion's San Francisco compound. This was a chink in her armor that he would make the most of.

To be savagely honest with himself, it wouldn't exactly be a distasteful task. She was the most desirable woman he'd met in a long time. If things had been different, he'd be thinking about getting her into bed right about now. But things weren't different, and he had no intention of going that far. Fortunately he had the advantage over her because he knew with near-certainty who she really was.

Now he had the means of removing any last, lingering doubt about Cathy Prentiss's identity. Both Emily and Frank Kampion's fingerprints were on file with the bureau.

He turned from the window, jerked open a drawer and removed a plastic Ziploc bag from the box. After carrying it to the table, he picked up the mug Cathy had used, gingerly gripping it at its base between thumb and index finger. He dropped the mug in the bag and closed it securely.

He could have waited until morning and called Agent Brown's office to request a courier to pick up the bag and deliver it to whatever lab the locals used. Instead, seized by a restlessness he didn't understand, he opted to walk to Brown's home and hand it to him in person.

Angel had barely opened her eyes Monday morning when she wanted to go to Darrin's apartment for an ice cream bar. "He *said* I could come anytime," she kept repeating.

"You haven't even had your breakfast," Cathy said.

"Can I go after breakfast?"

"No. Darrin is working and you mustn't disturb him."

"But he said—"

"No, Angel."

Angel pouted, but Cathy ignored her, wishing that Angel had never met the man, regretting that she'd taken her to his apartment Sunday afternoon. She didn't want Angel to become too attached to a virtual stranger living in Charlotte Amalie only temporarily. Wisdom dictated that she steer clear of Darrin Boyle, too. She avoided investigating why being in close quarters with the man set off all her body's alarm mechanisms.

Angel was still in a bad mood when Cathy delivered her to Gwen's apartment and left for work. Angel's crankiness all morning had done nothing to sweeten Cathy's mood, either.

Even Lyle Wenger noticed. He came upon Cathy unexpectedly as she was sorting through records of sales filled out by the eighteen-year-old art student who worked in the gallery on weekends.

"You're scowling." Lyle's voice made her jump. She hadn't known he'd entered the office.

"It's Bradley's handwriting. They should go back to teaching penmanship in school." She thrust a sales ticket at Lyle. "Look. Is that four hundred or seven hundred?"

"Four." He handed it back to her with a grin. Lyle was tall and blond, with a craggy face. He looked at least five years younger than his forty years. "My theory is that Bradley is secretly training to be a doctor. He's practicing his prescription-writing technique." When this didn't elicit a trace of a smile, he added, "You feeling okay? You can go home if you're not. I can handle things this afternoon."

"I feel fine," she snapped, then tried to soften the impact of her tone by adding, "Don't mind me. I had a bad weekend. To finish things off, Angel got up in a foul mood this morning."

"Maybe you should start spending some time with adults occasionally—preferably male adults."

She gazed at him and decided he wasn't necessarily casting himself as one of those males. He was simply showing a little friendly concern. She'd never felt pressured in any way by Lyle, and she didn't now. In fact, she was tempted to tell him that she'd spent a brief period with a male adult on Sunday and it hadn't brightened her weekend.

"Not yet," she said simply.

"It's been a year," he said gently, echoing Gwen's recent observation. The bell attached to the gallery's entrance door tinkled.

She shrugged. "I guess it doesn't feel that long. Maybe when Angel starts school..."

He raised a brow and shook his head, as though washing his hands of her, and went to greet the customer.

All in all, it was a slow, depressing afternoon. Instead of four hours, Cathy felt she'd spent eight hours at the gallery that day with little to occupy her, which left her thoughts free to ramble down treacherous roads. For instance, had Darrin Boyle really needed her to tell him where to hang the watercolors, or was that only an excuse to get her in his apartment? How had he gotten that scar over his upper lip? Had the thought of kissing her gone through his mind as they stood close together in his kitchen and brushed a lock of hair off her cheek?

At the stroke of five o'clock, Cathy grabbed her purse and left the gallery, calling "See you tomorrow," over her shoulder to Lyle.

When she arrived at Gwen's apartment, Dawn and Angel were sharing an after-school snack of graham crackers and milk with first-grader Eric.

"You look tired," Gwen told Cathy. "Sit down and have a cup of tea with me while Angel finishes her snack."

Cathy sank into a chair with a sigh and put her head back while Gwen brewed tea, then carried the tea tray into the living room, setting it on a low table between them.

"I know you don't like Angel to snack this late since you like to get dinner over with early," Gwen said. "But the girls just woke up from their naps fifteen minutes ago. I took them to the beach after lunch, and they wore themselves out romping with Darrin Boyle." She handed Cathy a teacup. "Now that's a sexy man. He surely enjoys children, too, although he said he hasn't any of his own."

Cathy stirred her tea slowly to cool it, hoping her face didn't reveal the consternation she was feeling. "Darrin Boyle went to the beach with you?"

"Oh, no." Gwen lifted her cup daintily and took a sip. "He was already there when we arrived. You should have seen Angel's eyes light up when she saw him." She eyed Cathy calculatedly over the rim of her cup. "She told me that the two of you went to Darrin's apartment yesterday."

"He wanted me to tell him where to hang the watercolors he bought at the gallery," Cathy said a bit defensively. "We were there less than fifteen minutes."

"Well, Angel is enchanted with the man. After today, so is Dawn. He played with them for over an hour. Helped them build a sand castle. Let them bury him in the sand."

"What were you doing while all this was going on?"

Gwen smiled somewhat sheepishly. "I confess I caught a few winks under the shade of a tree. I didn't get much sleep last weekend."

An anxious frown creased Cathy's brow. "Don't you think it's odd for an attractive, apparently single man to spend his time at the beach playing with other people's children?"

Gwen's mouth dropped open and her teacup rattled as she set it in its saucer. "Good heavens, Cathy, you aren't suggesting there's something perverted about the man!"

Cathy shook her head, meaning it. That particular worry had never entered her mind. Still, she thought Gwen had acted negligently, and she was very disappointed in her. "No, I'm just saying it's . . . unusual. If he's so crazy about kids, why isn't he married and having children of his own?"

Gwen raked her fingers through her thick, auburn hair, looking bewildered. "I guess he hasn't found the right woman. Cathy, you're overprotective. You'll smother Angel. Hey, you're really angry, aren't you?"

"I suppose I am," Cathy admitted. "I'm disappointed that you would take Angel out and turn her over to a virtual stranger."

Gwen sat back in her chair, obviously amazed at Cathy's reaction. "I didn't turn her over and, anyway, he's not a stranger. He lives in this building. He's a very nice man."

"You don't know that for a fact. You only met the man—what, two and a half weeks ago? He could be another Jack the Ripper, for all you know."

Gwen uttered a startled laugh. "I'm a darned good judge of men. I'm sure you don't need to worry about Darrin Boyle."

"Gwen," Cathy said earnestly, wanting to impress her with the seriousness of her concern, "when you first started baby-sitting Angel, you promised you'd clear it with me first when you wanted to take her away from the apartment."

"Good Lord, I'd almost forgotten that. Honey, I decided to take them to the beach on the spur of the moment. Frankly, it didn't even occur to me to call you. I thought, well, when you asked me for that promise, I thought it was because you didn't know me well enough at first to trust me completely. But surely now—"

"It has nothing to do with my trusting you," Cathy said. "I simply don't want Angel exposed to...to unnecessary danger."

"Danger!" Gwen rose and walked behind her chair. She gripped its back, clearly struggling not to lose her temper. "That's insulting, Cathy."

"I didn't mean—"

"No. What you're really saying is that I'm too incompetent to keep an eye on Angel outside the walls of this apartment."

"I'm not saying that at all," Cathy insisted. Now was not the time to remind Gwen that she'd fallen asleep at the beach.

"Then what the hell are you saying?"

"Maybe I am overprotective...."

The half-hearted admission didn't apply any oil to the troubled waters. Gwen had the legendary redhead's quick temper, but Cathy had never been its target before. She had truly hurt Gwen's feelings, and she hadn't meant to do that at all.

"Look, if you can't trust me to take care of Angel, maybe you should find somebody else."

"Oh, Gwen, don't say that. Of course, I trust you."

"It doesn't sound like it," Gwen shot back.

Months ago, Cathy had known that this moment might come. It was only natural that Gwen hadn't expected the promise to hold indefinitely. She hadn't treated Angel any differently than she treated her own children.

In the beginning, Cathy had fabricated a story to tell Gwen if it ever became necessary. Having already lied to Gwen by saying her husband was dead, she hated to add to that lie. But she didn't think she would be able to soothe Gwen's feelings any other way. And Angel's safety came first, even if she had to pile lie upon lie to convince Gwen.

"It's not that I'd mind your taking Angel to the beach under...other circumstances. And I'm not really that concerned about Darrin Boyle." Well, she was, but not for the reason she'd given Gwen. "There's something I've never told you and I guess it's time I did."

Gwen was still stiff with indignation, but she sat back down in her chair. She clasped her hands on her knees and waited for Cathy to continue.

"After my husband died, his parents tried to get custody of Angel. They never really liked me, you see, and they said—maybe they had really convinced themselves it was true—they said that I hadn't worked since I married and was incapable of providing for Angel."

Gwen's posture relaxed as she listened to Cathy's words. "They could have contributed to your support."

"They could have offered. I wouldn't have accepted. But it was simply a way to justify their determination to take Angel away from me. My husband was an only child, and after he died they became obsessed with Angel. They filed a custody suit. I ran away."

"But they couldn't have gotten Angel! They'd have had to prove you were unfit!"

"I know that, and I think I could have gone through the court proceedings if I'd thought that would be the end of it. I didn't believe it would be. For one thing, they'd probably have been granted visitation rights. I couldn't let that happen. I truly believe that if they'd ever been allowed to take Angel out of our home, they'd have disappeared with her and I'd never have seen her again. I'm sure they hired a private investigator to find us when we disappeared. I believe they're still looking, even now. They aren't the sort of people ever to give up, and they have the money to pursue the investigation indefinitely. So, if I seem overprotective..."

"Dear God in heaven," Gwen breathed when Cathy's voice trailed off. "How perfectly horrible for you." She sat forward and grasped Cathy's hands. "No wonder you're upset with me for falling asleep and leaving Angel exposed in a public place. I wish you'd told me this sooner."

"I—I didn't want to burden you with my problems."

"Believe me, I'll be more alert after this." She made a wry face. "I'll probably see private detectives around every corner for a while."

"I don't mean to frighten you. Just keep close to Angel when you take her out, and try to avoid crowds when she's with you."

"Of course I will, honey." Gwen was all sympathy now, which made Cathy feel even more wretched about deceiving her. But it couldn't be helped. The danger of Angel being kidnapped was very real, even though it would be her father who was behind it, not her grandparents. In fact, three of Angel's grandparents were dead and Frank's mother had never shown much interest in Angel. She worked at keeping her figure and looking young, and Cathy had always suspected she resented Frank and Cathy for making her a grandmother.

"You should have a gun," Gwen said.

Cathy's mind snapped back to the conversation. "No. I hate guns."

"Think it over," Gwen advised. "I have one. Just knowing it's there makes me feel safer. I bought it in a pawn shop."

Cathy was disconcerted by Gwen's words. "Where do you keep it?"

"Locked up in my bedside table."

"Could you really shoot someone?"

"Oh, yes. If somebody broke into my apartment, I wouldn't hesitate."

Cathy shivered involuntarily. "Well, I don't want to buy one. I'd have to register it. I don't want my name on any legal document in St. Thomas."

Gwen nodded. "Afraid the grandparents would pick up the paper trail? That's not likely, is it?"

"Still . . ."

"There are other ways to get a gun," Gwen mused. "Jeremy would know where to go. There are few permanent residents of the Virgins that he doesn't know, or know of."

A momentary flicker of interest made Cathy hesitate. If she could get a gun without having to sign her name . . .

"Just think about it," Gwen repeated.

Chapter 5

Darrin didn't emerge from his apartment the next four days, except during the hours when he knew Cathy was at work. Even then, he used the front entrance to his wing, where he was less likely to run into Gwen Nettleton or the children. The meeting at the beach Monday afternoon had been accidental. He'd have preferred not to spend time with Cathy's daughter so soon after Sunday, but once the meeting had occurred, he'd made the most of it.

He'd wormed his way a little deeper into Angel's heart. That was how he thought of it, in spite of his efforts not to do so. After all, his job was to gain Cathy's trust and how better do that then to charm her daughter?

He'd known Cathy would hear of it, which was why he'd made himself scarce the past few days. He feared now that he'd moved too quickly Sunday afternoon when he'd asked Cathy to help him hang the paintings. He'd had plenty of time to worry that she'd seen through that tissue-thin excuse, had realized he'd simply wanted her on his home ground for however long she would stay.

Which hadn't been long, but long enough for him to make an incredibly stupid blunder and ask about her husband. Long enough for him to sense that he frightened her. Because she was attracted to him, he'd told himself at the time, and his touching her had brought that attraction too close to the surface and she'd realized that he posed an emotional threat. Any woman married to Frank Kampion would have to be suicidal to think about even looking at another man.

With the hindsight of several days, he now wondered if he'd read her correctly. Maybe she was frightened of him because she still entertained doubts that their meeting and his moving into her apartment building were as innocent as they seemed. If so, his presence at the beach Monday afternoon when Angel arrived with Gwen, must have strengthened those doubts. How many coincidences could she swallow, after all?

He'd finally decided that he'd better back away from Cathy Prentiss and her daughter for a while. He forced himself to type and print out more pages of Kent's computer book each morning, but he was restless enough to jump out of his skin at the slightest provocation. It didn't help that the local police lab, where Brown had taken the mug Cathy had handled, was in no hurry to report back.

He called Brown every day. "They work on their own time schedule over there," Brown kept explaining, "and they're shorthanded."

"We could have mailed both sets of fingerprints to Washington and had them back by now," Darrin had said Thursday afternoon the third time he'd called Brown.

"They've no idea it's urgent. I made sure of that. They don't know whose fingerprints I asked them to check that mug against. You made it a point to remind me that the fewer people who know what's going on here, the better." Not that I needed reminding, his tone clearly said.

"I know, I know. I'm antsy."

"She's not going anywhere as long as she feels safe."

"Sorry to bother you," Darrin said and hung up. Brown was right. Cathy didn't suspect her cover was blown. If she did, she'd have run before now. There was even a chance that there was no cover and that the fingerprints wouldn't match. A slim chance, and he recognized that part of his impatience was due to an urgency to remove it finally. One way or the other.

His phone rang at four o'clock Friday afternoon. Despite his impatience to know the results of the lab comparison, he hesitated for a few seconds before answering. Maybe it's Rainey, he thought as he lifted the receiver.

It was Brown. "They match," he said, a barely restrained excitement in his voice.

"There's no doubt?"

"None. They lifted a complete thumbprint off the mug."

"Thanks."

"Sure. Uh, well, if you need anything else." He sounded deflated. He must have expected more in the way of a response from Darrin. Maybe he hoped Darrin would discuss the case with him, now that they knew they'd found Emily Kampion. Maybe he'd even hoped Darrin would involve him in the investigation, if in a minor role.

"Thanks again, Brown," Darrin said crisply and hung up. He should have been elated, and he wondered why he wasn't. Maybe because Brown's information was anticlimactic. He hadn't really doubted that he'd found Kampion's wife, had he? It wasn't possible that somewhere inside of him there had been a buried hope that the prints wouldn't match.

Hell, no. After a year of trying to find a clue as to where the biggest drug kingpin on the West Coast might surface, he'd finally succeeded. The agency had been trying for years to accumulate enough evidence to try Kampion on drug trafficking charges. They'd even found a few witnesses who'd agreed to testify against the man. All but one of them had disappeared or met with fatal "accidents." The lone surviving witness was in hiding with a new identity. He now seemed reluctant to testify. And who could blame him?

A year ago, in frustration, the bureau had pulled together a case against Kampion, charging him with income tax evasion. Comparison of income reported to the IRS with Kampion's extravagant life-style would go a long way toward convincing a judge and jury, and they had other evidence, as well. If they could put the man behind bars, the reluctant witness might then be willing to testify against Kampion on a trafficking charge, which would carry a far more severe penalty. But Kampion had a terrific information network. He'd been tipped off to the income tax charges and had disappeared before an arrest could be made. When agents arrived at the Kampion compound outside San Francisco, Kampion, his wife and child were gone.

Now that any lingering doubt about Cathy's identity had been removed, Kampion, when he did show up, wouldn't be able to slip through Darrin's grasp this time, no matter what he called himself or how altered his appearance was. There was a good chance he'd had plastic surgery—maybe several times in the past year—and he'd look very different. It didn't matter.

Darrin stared at the phone for a moment, knowing that he'd catch hell if he didn't report in to Rainey immediately. He shrugged and turned away. Rainey didn't even know a fingerprint comparison was being made, and what Rainey didn't know couldn't make him blow a gasket.

He had more urgent matters on his mind than Rainey's blood pressure. It was time he made contact with Mrs. Frank Kampion again, he thought grimly. Better yet, that she made contact with him.

He kept an eye on the back entrance to A-wing for the rest of the afternoon. At five o'clock, he carried a beer and a paperback suspense novel out of his terrace and made himself comfortable in a metal-framed, webbed longue he dragged over from near the pool.

About a quarter after, Angel ran across the back lawn without even seeing him. Keeping his head lowered, as though reading, he peeked over the top of his book. Gwen Nettleton stood near the door to A-wing, watching Angel. Then she waved and went back inside. Darrin surmised that Angel had run to meet her mother and that, after seeing Cathy approaching, Gwen had returned to her own apartment.

A few moments later, Cathy and Angel came into view from the other direction. As soon as he caught sight of them from the corner of his eye, he quickly lowered his gaze and stared at the open book.

He heard them talking, as they neared his terrace, but he didn't look up until Angel cried, "Hi, Darrin!" She released her mother's hand and ran up to the terrace. Her hair was done up in pigtails, tied with yellow ribbons to match her sunsuit. "What're you doing?"

Darrin feigned a surprised grin and lowered his book. "What's it look like, big'n?" He let his eyes drift to Cathy and called hello.

Angel came over to stand beside the longue. "Is that a good book?"

Darrin tweaked a pigtail. "Pretty good."

Angel giggled and pulled the pigtail out of his grasp. "I haven't seen you in a long, long time. Where have you been?"

"Right here, working hard." He looked up as Cathy walked to the terrace. "How are you, Cathy?"

She gave him a tired smile. "Pooped at the moment. Three cruise ships docked this afternoon and I swear every single passenger came into the gallery. Not all at the same time, fortunately."

"Mommy was going to take me to town and we were going to eat hot dogs and everything, but she's too tired," Angel said forlornly.

"I could take her," he offered and sensed as much as saw Cathy stiffen. Clearly she still didn't trust him.

Angel spun around to face her mother and hopped up and down. "Can I, Mommy? Can I, please?"

Cathy was already shaking her head. "No, Angel. Not today."

"But why not? Why won't you let me go?" Angel wheedled.

"Angel, don't argue."

"Today's probably not a good time, after all," Darrin said hastily. "Maybe one afternoon next week while your mother's at work—"

"Absolutely not."

He could see that she regretted her adamant tone immediately, but not the refusal. She definitely didn't trust him. For whatever reason. That was something he was going to have to change.

"Mommy—" Angel began.

"I have a better idea," Darrin cut in before the tears started to fall. "I'm going to grill myself a hamburger after a while." He gave Cathy a laid-back smile. "Would you and Angel join me?"

"Oh, I don't know. I'm so tired—"

"You won't have to raise a finger. And you can leave whenever you want."

Angel clasped her small hands together excitedly. "Please, please, *please*, Mommy."

Darrin laughed and, after a moment, Cathy joined in. "Okay, already." She shook her head helplessly. "What time do you want us, Darrin?"

"How is seven?"

"Perfect," Cathy said. "That gives me time to catch my breath and bathe Angel."

Angel took her mother's hand and skipped along beside her toward A-wing, content to go as long as they were coming back. Five minutes after their arrival at the apartment, Gwen knocked at the door. "Where's Angel?" she whispered as she stepped inside.

"In her room."

"Good." Gwen handed Cathy a small brown paper sack.

"What's this?" Cathy thrust her hand in the sack and brought out a small, chrome handgun. It was cold and hard and somehow menacing.

"Gwen!"

"Shh," Gwen hissed. "Jeremy got it. He doesn't even know who I wanted it for. I told him it was for a friend who lives alone."

"I wouldn't know what to do with it."

"If somebody tries to take Angel away from you, you'll figure it out soon enough. Look, I have to get back home."

Gwen left and Cathy stared at the gun until she heard Angel running down the hall toward the living room. Quickly, she thrust the gun and sack into the nearest concealment, at the back of a drawer in the walnut secretary.

Cathy didn't feel at all guilty about relaxing in the longue on Darrin's terrace while he prepared the meal. She'd showered and dressed in a fresh skirt and blouse, not even bothering to wear a bra and slip because the day's heat usually lingered through early evening. The stone-washed denim skirt and tailored pink cotton blouse were heavy enough to hide the fact that she wore nothing beneath them except a pair of silk panties.

Lifting her hair off her neck, she put her head back against the longue and let her eyes drift closed. She could hear Darrin going and returning from his kitchen, carrying cloth and napkins, dishes and silverware to the small redwood table on the terrace. Angel trotted at his heels, "helping" and chattering like a magpie. Darrin's much deeper voice responded goodnaturedly. The smell of meat being grilled over charcoal floated in the air.

She had fallen into a light sleep when she felt Darrin's fingers curl gently over her shoulder. "Soup's on."

She sat up abruptly, shaking off his hand, but its heat remained, burning through her cotton blouse. "I was asleep," she said, hardly believing it herself. "I'm sorry."

"Don't be. You needed it."

Raking a hand through her tousled hair, she rose from the longue. Angel was already seated at the table, a napkin tucked under her chin. "I made the salad, Mommy," she announced, "all by myself."

"Good for you," Cathy said.

There was a moment of embarrassment for Cathy when she placed her hand on the back of a chair and his hand came down on top of it. She jerked her hand back, realizing that he only meant to pull the chair out for her. She felt flushed and was grateful for the cover of dusky twilight.

This is a mistake, she thought. I don't even know how to act around an attractive man. That wasn't exactly true, she mused as she sat down. She knew that the wise course, the only course for her, was not to get herself into situations like this. If she were somebody else, truly a widow whose most serious concerns were making ends meet and raising her daughter, she would be pleased he'd invited her to dinner, hoping that he found her attractive, that he would want to see her again without her daughter.

Darrin was behaving in a perfectly normal manner, but she felt an alarming tension whenever he came near her, a tension she hoped he was unaware of. "This looks wonderful," she said as Darrin sat down. "I love baked beans."

"They're from a deli," Darrin admitted. "I grill steaks and burgers and scramble eggs. Beyond that I depend on somebody else's cooking."

"I can make cookies and salads," Angel announced in a clear attempt to draw Darrin's attention back to her.

"Cookies?" Darrin inquired. "Am *I* glad to hear that." He served Angel a spoonful of beans and himself several. "That's a hint, big'n, in case you didn't recognize it." He handed the bowl of beans to Cathy.

Angel was looking at him with her head cocked to one side. "What?"

"I think he'd like you to make him some cookies," Cathy told her.

She beamed. "Okay. Would you put some mustard on my bun?"

Cathy reached for the mustard container. "I want Darrin to do it," Angel said.

Cathy gave him an apologetic look and handed over the mustard. While he fixed Angel's hamburger to her satisfaction and cut it in half for her, Cathy applied herself to her own dinner.

"Which do you like better?" Angel was saying. "Chocolate chip or brownies?"

"A hard choice, but I'd have to say brownies."

Cathy marveled at the way this childless man had with children. Maybe he had younger siblings or nieces and nephews. Where had he lived as a child? she wondered. What kind of family did he have? Why had he never married? But maybe he had. He'd told Gwen that he had no children, not that he hadn't married. She realized that she was very curious about him and knew that she couldn't afford to be. Knowing more about him would only make her feel more comfortable with him, which would be foolish.

It was fortunate that Angel seemed bent on claiming his attention. The more those penetrating eyes were fastened on Angel, the less they would be on her.

The meal passed without Cathy having to contribute much to the conversation. Afterward, feeling guilty about falling asleep earlier, she insisted on helping clear the table. Fortunately, Angel didn't insist on "helping," which would only have slowed things down.

After placing the last dish in the dishwasher, she turned to Darrin, who was putting the leftovers in the refrigerator. "Thank you for dinner," she said. "I really didn't feel up to cooking tonight. Now I'd better take Angel home and put her to bed."

The refrigerator door closed with a soft thud as he straightened with a bottle in his hand. "I was hoping you'd stay long enough for a drink." He held up the bottle of red wine. "You aren't going to make me drink this all by myself, are you?"

It might have been his easy, boyish smile. Despite what her better judgment told her, it gave her a fluttery feeling in her stomach. Or it might have been the disappointment that was evident in his hazel eyes. It might even have been her perverse reluctance to accept his hospitality, eat his food, and then leave with an abruptness that bordered on rudeness.

Whatever the reason, she felt her resolve weakening and said, "No, I couldn't let you do that. Where are the glasses?"

"On the top shelf to the right of the sink."

She got the glasses and took a few seconds to brace herself. Only a few minutes more, for the sake of politeness, and she and Angel could go. She could probably depend on Angel to draw his attention away from her, as she'd done at dinner.

She blinked as she stepped out on the terrace. After the lighted kitchen, it seemed much darker than before. Angel was curled in the longue, asleep.

"Over here," Darrin said quietly. Turning, she saw that he had placed pads from the redwood chairs on the grass near the terrace and was already sitting on one of them, leaning back against the low wall that enclosed the terrace, his blue-jeaned legs stretched out in front of him.

Hesitating only briefly, she walked across the terrace, circling around the low wall, and sat down beside him. The night was perfumed by the heavy scent of angel's-trumpets. He took the glasses and for the space of a full minute, it seemed there was nothing but the sound of the wine being poured.

Anything was better than this throbbing silence, she thought, and when he handed her a glass, she asked, "Have you ever been married?"

He didn't answer immediately, but seemed to be studying her face. She couldn't read his expression. They were beyond the reach of the lighted kitchen windows. The dipping lawn in front of them and the clumps of low shrubbery seemed swaddled in soft, dark velvet. All she could see of the swimming pool was the glimmering surface, like a sheet of tinted glass reflecting distant circles of light.

"No," he murmured.

She settled back against the wall and lifted her glass. The wine was a sharp coolness in her mouth sliding down to become a pleasant warmth in her stomach. "I'm surprised." As she spoke, Cathy watched the circles of light reflected in the pool quivering gently. "You're the sort of man who should be married."

He settled back beside her, his shoulder grazing hers. "You mean I need somebody to clear out the clutter in my apartment and save me from deli meals?"

She laughed a little. "I didn't mean that. I've noticed that you're very good with children, that's all."

"I like kids. I always have. They're so honest."

She darted a glance at his shadowed face, then turned back to stare at the pool and sip her wine. Was there a subtle hint in his words that perhaps *she* had been less than honest with him? No, of course not. She was merely feeling guilty about the lies she had to tell. Her life, her very name, were lies.

"I was engaged once," he said.

"What happened?"

"I got cold feet. As the wedding date approached, I started noticing things about her that I'd never seen before."

Leaning forward, she pulled her knees up beneath her skirt and settled her chin on them. "What sort of things?"

"She was miserly. She saved buttons and string, for God's sake. She let me know she considered herself a better money manager than I and I was supposed to bring my check home and hand it over. She'd pay the bills and handle our investments, which would amount to a tidy sum in no time if I'd limit my spending to the piddling allowance she was prepared to give me. To be fair, hers was just as piddling. The scales fell from my eyes in the nick of time. She loved money. Not what it would buy, but the idea of it, sitting there in stocks and bonds and bank accounts, compounding. It turned her on."

She smiled in the darkness, unable to imagine any woman thinking she could put him on such a short leash. "I had a great-uncle who was like that. He denied himself and his family all his life and ended up old and alone and unloved. Then he died and left piles of money to his children, who squandered it as though there was no tomorrow." For a moment she lowered her forehead to her knees, having suddenly realized that she was revealing things about herself. But surely a great-uncle whom she could barely remember was a safe enough topic of conversation. She lifted her head and settled her chin back on her knees. "I can remember my parents talking about it. I must've been about ten at the time."

He took the glass from her fingers to refill it, then handed it back. I've had enough wine, she told herself. I shouldn't even be here. But the soft, scented night lulled her anxieties. Her eyes brooded on the pool and a dreamy softness crept through her.

He penetrated it with his next words. "Where do your parents live?"

Perhaps she should go now before she said anything more. Every lie she told made her feel a little sadder. And then she realized that there was no reason to lie in the present instance. What harm could it do to tell him the truth about her parents? "I had a brother, four years older than I. He died on a motorcycle when he was eighteen. My mother was inconsolable, and she never could seem to put his death behind her. She took an overdose of sleeping pills when I was sixteen. I'll never know if it was an accident or not."

His hand was halfway to her hair before he stopped himself. "And your father?"

"He died of a massive coronary when I was in my senior year at college." She had felt abandoned. For a while she'd been angry with her father for dying and leaving her without any family at all. She'd been even angrier at herself for not being there when he died.

Somehow she'd managed to concentrate on her studies until graduation. Equipped with a degree in art history, she'd landed a job at a San Francisco art museum, and that was where she met Frank. He'd donated a large sum of money to remodel one wing of the museum. It had been reopened with an invitation-only champagne reception in Frank's honor. She had first seen him standing beneath a landscape by Gainsborough, in a white dinner jacket, his wavy hair as black as his trousers. He was the envy of every man in the room, a business entrepreneur whose every venture made him richer, it was believed.

Frank Kampion was the most sophisticated, self-assured man she'd ever known, and she was young and lonely. She had been ripe to be swept off her feet by such a man, and they were married less than a year later.

The unhappiness in her voice hit Darrin hard, like an unexpected blow to the back that left you without breath in your lungs. It could not have been feigned. She had told him the truth about her family. He sat still and forced himself to look at it objectively. What did the truth about her parents and her brother cost her? And what did it gain him? Nothing. From the information in her file, he knew that it had happened before she ever met Frank Kampion. As far as the bureau file was concerned, her history started on that day; there was no mention of anything before that.

Very deliberately he plucked a few blades of grass and let them fall between his fingers. "And then you lost your husband."

She emptied her wineglass and turned toward him. "Yes." In a very real sense it was true. The day she picked up the extension phone in the bedroom and overheard Frank making arrangements for the delivery of a planeload of cocaine, she had lost the man she'd loved, in fact discovered that that man had never existed at all except in her imagination. At first she had tried to deny it, tried to tell herself that she'd misunderstood. But when she'd confronted him, he'd admitted that his fortune had been earned in drug trafficking, not in legitimate business ventures. His various corporations were blinds for the real business he conducted.

She might have contrived to believe him for a time, at least, if he'd lied, but he hadn't even given her that. He had thought it amusing that it had taken four years for her to figure things out, when the evidence was all around her.

"What about your husband's family? Do you see them?"

Deep inside her, truth struggled with sanity. She banked it down in an instant before it was too late. He couldn't help her. Nobody could. He couldn't even begin to understand.

"No," she said shortly. "They tried to take Angel away from me." She started to stand, but the hand on her arm stopped her.

She turned to say she had to go and found his face inches from hers. Though shadows lay in the hollows of his cheeks and along one side of his nose, she could see him clearly now. His eyes were fixed on hers, dark, intense, and she realized it was the intensity of desire, hot and restless. And something in her stirred in response. She was afraid.

He pulled her closer and she resisted, putting her hands on his chest.

"No. I don't want this." But, God in heaven, she did want it, wanted him.

His mouth lowered, touched hers, and she didn't turn away. In an instant, fear and insanity were swept away by a flood of passion. The taste of his mouth aroused such a fierce, wild need in her that she forgot who she was and why she couldn't allow this to mean something to her. She was at sea in roiling desire. His tongue probed, languidly searching, while his lips alternately seduced and crushed hers, making reckless demands that would not be denied. Her fingers dove into his hair and she gripped his hard face and answered, kiss for kiss, groan for groan, need for need.

He tore his mouth from hers to move over her face, tasting and absorbing the texture of her skin. Her head reeled, and she was wild to have his mouth on hers again. She whimpered helplessly, turning her head blindly in search of his lips.

He answered her plea by crushing his mouth down on hers again. His hands found their way beneath her blouse, up the satin planes of her back, then around to possess the soft weight of her unfettered breasts. A moan was wrenched from him and lost in the wet, winey delights of her mouth.

As he lowered her to lie in the grass, the night breeze felt cool on the fevered flesh of her face and on the slender arms that had wrapped themselves around his neck. She felt the hard weight of his body and his lips moving against hers, though she didn't understand his muttered words. They sounded fierce and desperate somehow, almost angry.

She was unaware of Angel stirring in her sleep on the longue on the other side of the terrace. There was only the sweet-smelling grass beneath her and his lips and hands now.

With a groan, he buried his face in her throat, feeding the fire that was already roaring out of control.

"Darrin." Was that feeble whisper of sound her voice?

Roughly, he caught her bottom lip between his teeth, drawing it into his mouth, and she forgot what she had meant to say.

"Mommy..."

They froze, the sounds of their labored breathing loud in the night silence. Cathy could hear her heart pumping furiously in her ears. Had Angel called? She moved her arm and felt grass. It was as if her mind had gone off somewhere and suddenly it rushed back into her body. She was lying on the grass with Darrin. Her blouse was open and her nipples tingled from the touch of his fingers. She had been kissing him with a savage hunger that she'd never felt in her life before.

With a muffled cry, she pushed at him and he rolled off her, springing up before his slowly returning reason deserted him again. She sat up, clutching the front of her blouse together, fumbling with buttons and fighting tears.

Darrin drew air into his lungs deeply, looking away from her until the heat that radiated through him began to cool. He had come that close to taking her. He was out of his mind. He heard her erratic breathing and when he risked looking at her, she was getting to her feet, poking the tail of her blouse into the waistband of her skirt.

My God, what a colossal disaster. "Cathy—"

"Don't say anything, not a word." Her voice was unsteady and she wouldn't look at him. Then, lifting her chin, she brushed by him and walked to the chaise longue where Angel still lay.

Cathy looked down at her sleeping daughter. Thank God she had merely cried out in her sleep. She was probably getting chilled. She wasn't aware that Darrin had moved until he spoke softly, close behind her.

"I'll carry her home."

She wheeled on him angrily. "No," she said sharply. "I don't want you to carry her."

She bent and lifted the child in her arms, shifting Angel's weight against her. Angel's head dropped to her shoulder, her legs dangled down. The child was obviously a heavy burden for her, but he knew better than to offer his help again.

He stood back and let her pass and watched her struggle across the lawn under Angel's deadweight. He blocked out the nagging voice that told him he'd blown whatever chance he might have had to earn her trust.

Chapter 6

Darrin spent several minutes pacing his apartment, cursing himself. You damned fool, he fumed. Stupid, blundering damned fool. A distinct heaviness lingered in his groin area, and that made him even angrier.

He stormed into the bathroom, tore off his clothes and deliberately turned the cold shower on full blast. He stepped in and stood there, rigid, gritting his teeth and cursing some more, until he could stand the frigid pellet-hard spray without shaking.

Did he have to react like a sex-starved college freshman just because she had allowed him to kiss her? he asked himself furiously as his muscles began to relax and his teeth lost the need to clatter against each other. Did he have to wrestle her around in the grass and practically rip off her clothes? Did he have to want her with the kind of consuming desire that knew no reason?

Such unrestrained need for her—*for Frank Kampion's wife*, he reminded himself fiercely—was going to interfere with his investigation. To say the least of it.

Emily Kampion was a job, only a job. She was the bait in the trap he was setting for Kampion. If the man had had plastic surgery—and if Darrin were in Kampion's shoes, he would have done exactly that—it was possible Darrin wouldn't recognize him. He'd seen Kampion only once in person, and from some distance. And that had been the old Kampion who boldly went about San Francisco, playing the big business tycoon and patron of the arts.

So he needed Cathy. He couldn't think of her as Emily, even knowing who she was. He told himself that was good. If he kept thinking of her as Cathy, he wouldn't slip and call her Emily.

Any strange man who made contact with her would be suspect. He would be tailed until he was identified. They would know what brand of deodorant he used. He wouldn't be able to go to the john without being watched.

There was no margin for error; they had to be sure before they took him. If they picked up the wrong man, Cathy would be tipped off that she was under surveillance and they might never get Kampion. He had to overcome her mistrust and stick to her like a wet T-shirt until it was over.

An unfortunate simile, he thought grimly, remembering the feel of her naked breasts in his hands, the taut rigidity of the nipples when he touched them. He grabbed the soap and lathered himself roughly.

He wanted it to be over. She had lied to him again tonight, saying her husband's parents had tried to take Angel away. Kampion's father was dead. His mother was a social butterfly in Boston. Why the hell didn't he just call Rainey, tell him about the fingerprint match, and suggest they take Cathy in for questioning?

But he knew why. Rainey would raise cain. What if Cathy wouldn't talk? He could break her, Darrin thought, scrubbing his skin vigorously. He could *make* her tell him where Kampion was. Could you really? a mocking voice said in his head. Could you get tough with those deep blue eyes accusing you?

He was grasping at straws, anyway. It was entirely possible that she didn't know where her husband was holed up, that she'd merely been told to wait in St. Thomas until Kampion contacted her.

So he would keep on using her. Why he should have any qualms about doing whatever was necessary to resolve the investigation, he didn't know.

It would help if she wasn't so damned desirable. God, he'd really gotten into that kiss tonight. But so had she, not that he could draw any justification from that. If Angel hadn't called out in her sleep...

The thought of the child gave him a distinctly uncomfortable twinge. Angel. The name suited her. She was as pure and innocent as an angel, and he was trying to put her father away for...

No, he told himself. What he was doing was trying to save her from growing up in the world of racketeering and drug smuggling.

That was his job, and he couldn't let sympathy or sexual attraction for Cathy get in the way of doing it. She might seem vulnerable and in need of protection, but it was obvious from the dyed hair and false name that she knew law enforcement agencies were searching for her. And she lied as easily as she told the truth. She was practiced at deception.

He closed his eyes and rubbed the soap over his face. Maybe it would wash away the smell of green grass and the light scent of lilacs he'd discovered in the hollow of her throat.

Look at the bigger picture, he told himself. Think how many kids might be saved from the havoc wreaked by drugs if Kampion's operation could be destroyed.

Lying in the darkness of her bedroom, Cathy was fighting her own private battle, too tightly strung to sleep. Every time she saw Darrin, he managed to peel off another layer of her defenses. How had he gotten so close to her in so short a time?

She was sure he wasn't working for Frank. That was at least one worry she could forget, she told herself. To start with, he had signed a six-month apartment lease and, from all she'd seen, was exactly what he said he was. Furthermore, there had been ample opportunity for him to make off with Angel, if that were his intention. The afternoon at the beach when Gwen had fallen asleep would have been the ideal time. If he'd wanted both her and Angel, he'd had them at his mercy the day they went to his apartment. Tonight, as well.

This didn't mean she could allow herself to become involved with him. There was too much to over-come—too many lies, too many explanations she couldn't make. The only way she could be sure of staying hidden was to confide in no one, no matter how much she wanted to or how trustworthy that person seemed. One misjudgment on her part, and she could lose Angel for good. That was quite enough to worry about without complicating her life further by getting involved with Darrin Boyle.

Nothing else mattered. Not the wild passions that had engulfed her when he'd started making love to her tonight. Not the sick sense of loss she'd felt when she'd walked away from him, carrying Angel.

Curling into a fetal position, she tried to block out what had happened with Darrin. But then she could feel his hands on her breasts and his mouth plundering hers. It was madness.

Unable to bear the memories, she sprang out of bed. The dark bedroom felt like an airless prison. She went to the window and threw it wide open. Peeling off her damp cotton gown, she let the cool night air soothe her skin.

Then, she thought she saw a movement beside a clump of palm trees between the apartment building and the hotel. She froze and peered intently at the trees for a long time. Now nothing moved in the shadows. Nerves, she told herself. After a while, she felt her shattered equilibrium righting itself. She shut and locked the window and closed the blind.

What she really needed, she thought, was to go somewhere with Angel for a few days, just the two of them. Lyle had offered her the use of his condo on St. John more than once. Maybe she should take him up on it. He could get along without her at the gallery for a couple of days. She refused to examine the possibility that, more than a holiday, she needed time to whip her wayward emotions back into line before facing Darrin again.

"Boyle?" Brown's voice was uncertain.

Darrin hadn't answered until the fifth ring. He had been seriously debating not answering at all. He'd ignored the damned instrument's persistent ringing the past four days.

"Good afternoon, Brown. Catch any crooks today?"

Brown laughed halfheartedly, evidently unsure as to whether Darrin was joking or being sarcastic. "Not today. Listen, I thought I'd better warn you. Rainey called me, hopping mad. Says you haven't been answering your phone."

"I've been out of pocket," Darrin said uninformatively. "When did he call you?"

"Just now."

"What else did he say?"

"Wanted to know what was happening with you-know-who."

"And you said?"

"That he'd have to talk to the agent on the case. It's protocol."

Darrin smiled at Brown's sincerity, glad the young agent hadn't been intimidated by Rainey into talking out of school. "Thanks, Brown. Don't worry about it. I'll call him." He disconnected and immediately dialed the Washington number. He couldn't put it off any longer.

"Where have you been?" Rainey demanded as soon as Darrin identified himself. "I've been ringing your place every two hours."

"Out and around," Darrin said, knowing that kind of nonanswer infuriated Rainey. Before he could spill more invectives into the mouthpiece, Darrin added, "I'm calling now because there's been a new development. We lifted some of Catherine Prentiss's fingerprints off a coffee cup. It's a match."

A rare moment of silence on Rainey's end. "Well, it's about time." The news seemed to have knocked some of the force out of his anger.

Seizing the moment, Darrin said, "Still no sign of the husband, though." He paused, then added off-handedly, "We could put the local boys on her. When something starts to happen, they could handle it until I could get back. I have other work I should be doing, and this case could go on indefinitely."

"No it can't. What in hell is wrong with you, Boyle? What happened to 'This is *my* case'?"

Darrin sighed. He'd known Rainey wouldn't go for it. "I'm getting bored, old man. This hanging around makes me crazy."

"Then stop hanging around," Rainey snapped, "and concentrate on ingratiating yourself with the woman. Use that fabled charm I'm told you can turn on when you want to." He made a hacking sound into the phone, clearing his throat. "I can't see it myself."

"You're not my type."

"You don't give me palpitations, either. Call me back later in the week." He banged the receiver down without waiting for Darrin's agreement.

He'd known what he had to do, and he'd slowly come to grips with it during the hours since Friday night. But it irritated him to be issued a flat-out command. The criticisms in his progress file were right on target. He didn't like taking orders. He preferred to be left alone to do his job however he saw fit. Which he knew was an unrealistic preference in a government agency. At times, he thought he might eventually get so fed up with the bureaucracy, he'd resign and enter the private practice of law.

Restless, he dressed in running shorts and shoes and went out to sweat off his frustration. Returning to the complex an hour later, he saw Gwen Nettleton and her daughter on their terrace.

"Hi," he said, swiping his sweaty brow with the back of his hand. "Where's Angel?"

"They're gone."

His quick panic was as uncharacteristic as it was unprofessional. "Gone where?"

She sent him a shrewd look. "St. John. Cathy decided to take Angel for a holiday. They'll be back this evening. Cathy needed it. She's been looking harried lately and..." Gwen placed her hands on her hips and scowled at his retreating back. "Nice chatting with you, too," she muttered.

He slammed into his apartment and went straight to the bedroom for the lock picks. He didn't even take time to shower before circling the complex and entering A-wing through the front entrance. His blood was pumping furiously, and not from running. If he'd let her get away while he was holed up trying to get his damned head screwed on straight...

Moments later, he was in Cathy's apartment. He went into her bedroom, jerked open drawers and scanned the clothes in the closet. Then he checked Angel's room. When he'd searched the apartment previously, he'd made a mental inventory, and as he realized that the only items missing from their rooms were a couple of changes of clothes each, his panic began to fade.

A minimal amount of toiletries was missing from the bathroom medicine cabinet. "Okay," he muttered, as he let himself out of the apartment, "what next?"

In his own shower, he came up with a plan of action. He called the gallery, identified himself, and asked to speak with Cathy. "She's not here," a male voice said. "This is Lyle Wenger. May I take a message?"

"No." He schooled his voice to sound casual, offhand. "I was a little worried about her. I'm a neighbor and I haven't seen her since Friday."

"Oh, she needed a break. She's staying at my condo in St. John. I can give you the phone number if you like, but she's supposed to be back to work tomorrow."

"I'm relieved to hear it." Better not take the number. It would show too great an interest. "I'll wait and talk to her when she gets back. Sorry to bother you."

That was easy, he thought as he disconnected and dialed Brown's office. "Mrs. K. is staying in Lyle Wenger's condo in St. John."

"I can find out where it is for you in ten minutes."

"She's supposed to be back this evening. I don't want to be gone when she gets here but I want to know if anyone else is there besides her daughter."

"You mean she might be with...him?" Brown could barely contain his excitement. "I can go. The ferry at Red Hook Dock runs every hour."

"Good," Darrin bit out, hoping he wasn't making a mistake in turning Brown loose in St. John. But he had no other choice really. He couldn't be in two places at once. "When she leaves, go over every inch of that condo."

"Will do. If *he's* there, I won't let him get away. I'll report back soonest."

"Thanks," Darrin said and hung up.

He was too tense to do anything for the rest of the day but pace the kitchen and stare at the entrance to A-wing or roam the living room and stare at the telephone. Waiting was a big part of his job, and he wasn't very good at it.

What if she'd met Kampion and they'd disappeared from St. John before Brown got there? She'd left almost everything behind in the apartment, but the longer he thought about it, the more he feared that was a clever ruse. Her husband had enough money to replace it all, thousands of times over.

He was almost wild with frustration by the time Brown called at 9:00 p.m. "Did you see her?" Darrin barked before the agent could get into a convoluted report on his every move.

"Yes. She and the child left the condo at about six-thirty. She was carrying an overnight case. I tailed them to the dock. They got on the ferry to St. Thomas. I stayed until I saw it leave, to be sure."

Darrin's tense neck and back muscles began to loosen a little. His confidence in Brown had not been misplaced. Cathy should be back at the apartment now. She'd come in by the front entrance or he'd missed her on one of his nervous forays through the living room. "Good job, Brown."

"I'm calling from a pay phone near the condo. I've been over that place with a fine-tooth comb. There's an electric razor in the bathroom. The shirts in the closet have a fifteen neck size and the trousers belong to a pretty tall, thin dude. Thirty-one waist."

According to Kampion's file he was five-ten and muscled up from working with weights. His neck size was sixteen-and-a-half, his waist thirty-four. "They have to be Wenger's. Did you find anything else?"

"Nothing. I brought a fingerprint kit with me, and I picked up quite a few good prints. I'll leave them and Kampion's prints with the police lab tomorrow, but I don't think the guy's been here."

Darrin was aware of an enormous load sliding off his shoulders. He'd be willing to bet she hadn't met Kampion. If she had, why would she return to St. Thomas? "Try to get the lab to rush those comparisons."

"Okay. I have to run. The last ferry leaves at ten."

After hanging up, Darrin decided to go for a walk on the grounds and see if there were lights on in Cathy's apartment. It was a beautiful night. The black velvet sky was riddled with stars, and there was just enough breeze to cool the air. Hands stuffed in his trouser pockets, he forced himself to amble, rather than run, and whistled softly between his teeth. An ordinary guy out for an evening stroll.

He could see no lights through the closed blinds of her apartment, but she could have retired early. He knew he'd sleep better, though, if he had some proof that she was in there. As he ambled around the corner of A-wing, trying to decide whether to phone her and risk revealing his anxiety or wait until morning, the decision was taken out of his hands. As he neared her darkened terrace and realized someone was reclining in the redwood chaise, her voice called out, "Who's there?"

"Cathy?"

Suddenly she remembered standing at her open bedroom window Friday night, thinking that she'd seen a movement. She sat up quickly and peered into the darkness. "Darrin?"

He walked over to the chair next to the chaise longue and dropped into it. She slid her legs off the chaise, turning to sit sideways. Their knees were nearly touching. He could see her face now, its features blurred by the darkness.

"Are you all right?" He hadn't known he was going to ask the question. He hadn't known that concern for her was uppermost in his mind.

"Why wouldn't I be?" There had been real worry in his tone, and she tried not to think about what that meant. She had already decided this couldn't go any further, hadn't she?

"You were upset when you left Friday night. I was worried about you. I even called the gallery."

"You *what*?" To her amazement, she was suddenly, furiously angry. She didn't want him calling the gallery. She didn't want him to keep tabs on her.

"I wanted to talk to you, and you weren't answering your phone."

"You have no business checking up on me," she said thickly. Swiftly she shook her head to clear the mist from her eyes. What was wrong with her? Her emotions were too close to the surface. Don't fall apart, she told herself. His hand dropped to her hair, and swift despair made her tighten her hands into fists at her sides. Why couldn't she conquer the storm of feelings he aroused in her?

"I couldn't let things stand as we left them Friday night," he said quietly. "I lost my head for a few minutes, and I'm sorry."

"You're going to tell me it shouldn't have happened," she murmured, stunned at the enormous resentment she felt. Perhaps she resented it because she'd prepared something very much like that to say, and he'd beat her to it. What did she expect from the man? It *shouldn't* have happened, should it? "You were merely feeling sorry for the poor little widow and now you regret it, and I shouldn't get any wrong ideas.'' Gathering her resentment around her like a shield, she lifted her chin and looked straight at him. His eyes were narrowed, shadowed by brow and lashes, and she couldn't see their expression in the darkness.

His hand dropped to her shoulder. Let it go, he told himself, but he couldn't leave her like this. ''Sympathy had nothing to do with it,'' he said gently. ''I wanted you. I want you every time I'm near you.'' It was as though somebody else had taken over his vocal chords and was forcing the truth from his mouth. Rainey would applaud, say he was finally following orders and ingratiating himself. But he knew that the job was getting hopelessly mixed up with something that went much deeper, some bedrock down at the dark bottom of his soul.

There was nothing between them in that moment but his raw statement of fact. She knew that a part of her embraced the stark honesty of the words, but another part was desperately frightened by it. She could not love this man.

Love? Where had that come from? It was need she felt, the hungry need of a lonely woman for a man who stirred something reckless in her that she hadn't known was there. Simple animal need. Need she could understand. Need she could handle.

''Cathy.'' He took both her hands in his and felt her pulse speed instantly. He succeeded in banking down his unwilling response for only a moment before he dragged her to her feet and crushed her to him, devouring the sweetness of her mouth. He was instantly imprisoned in the softness, the fragrance, the need.

Cathy's head swam. She was being pulled in an ever-narrowing spiral toward a dark vortex of passion. It was the tiny, frantic voice at the back of her mind saying, *You can't lose control, it's too dangerous,* that gave her the strength to pull back on the very edge of the whirlpool.

"Darrin." She gripped his arms, holding tight while she tried to steady herself. After the space of several thundering heartbeats, she drew a deep breath and said, "Friday night . . . I wanted you, too, but now—"

"Now you don't?" he finished for her.

She stood with her head bowed, unable to speak.

"I don't believe you, Cathy."

She gathered her courage. "I was going to say that now I know I was feeling lonely and vulnerable Friday night. That's really why I went away for a couple of days. My life is too mixed up to add another complication right now. You—" she smiled ruefully "—are definitely a complication."

A delicate way of putting it, he thought grimly and muttered, "Because you still love your husband."

She looked up at him, but didn't speak for a moment. "I don't have a husband," she said finally, "but there are other problems. Angel's . . ." She found she couldn't say "grandparents," after all. She couldn't stand there touching him, and lie to him again. She didn't have the strength for it tonight.

She let her hands fall and stepped away from him. But the back of the chaise stopped her while she was still too close. "I'm tired. . . ."

He heard her sigh and wondered why she hadn't finished what she'd started to say, that Angel's grandparents were searching for her. Was it possible she was beginning to find it difficult to lie to him?

"You go to bed." He cupped her chin and kissed her deeply, but tenderly, before she could speak. "We'll talk later."

Chapter 7

He sat in his kitchen in the dark, nursing a beer, and thought of his options. He could request a transfer off the case, which would call for an explanation. He couldn't think of one that didn't sound like a flimsy excuse. The truth wouldn't do, either. If the agency suspected he was becoming emotionally involved with a gangster's wife, he'd be shipped to some backwater where he'd cool his heels until his retirement. If he didn't expire of boredom first.

He could resign and open a law practice. But some hard kernel of pride rejected that idea instantly. If ever he decided to leave the bureau, he preferred going out, if not in a blaze of glory, at least knowing that he would be missed. He didn't want any rumors, any hint of disgrace coloring his departure.

He knew, also, that he would always think a little less of himself if he walked away before he'd nailed Frank Kampion's hide to the wall.

He drained the beer can and set it down on the table, reminding himself that Cathy was, after all, a
gangster's wife who was getting too friendly with another man while her husband was holed up somewhere, hiding from the FBI and probably getting his
face fixed. True, she seemed upset by her attraction to
Darrin, but was she bothered enough to stay out of
temptation's way?

Not if he could help it, he thought with deliberate
harshness, and he suspected that he could. As she'd
admitted, she was lonely and vulnerable and probably
bored with playing the financially strapped, grieving
widow whose in-laws were out to steal her daughter
from her. Meanwhile she waited to hear from her husband, who was undoubtedly conducting business as
usual from some luxurious, secret base of operations.

Even as these calculated thoughts ran through his
mind, he hated the necessity of dismantling Cathy's
guilt and mistrust, brick by brick. She was not involved in any criminal activity, as far as he knew. What
if, after a year on the run, she'd taken a hard look at
her marriage, at where the money for her former ex-
pensive life-style came from? What if she would like to
get out?

Then he would help her. But she would have to confide in him.

She avoided him for the next two days. It was distressing not to be able to avoid thoughts of him, as
well. And disturbing questions. Was she strong enough
to live the rest of her life alone, except for Angel, pretending to be somebody else, always poised on the
panic edge of fear? She was only twenty-eight years old
and she had a young woman's needs. With a sinking

heart, she knew that it was unrealistic to expect she could deny them forever. But did she have any other choice?

Saturday morning, she awoke with a pounding tension headache. She disliked taking medication of any kind, but this time she knew she'd get no relief without it. She rolled out of bed and found the bottle of aspirin in the medicine cabinet.

The headache had subsided to a dull pain behind her eyes by the time she and Angel sat down to a breakfast of fruit and cold cereal.

"Mommy, can I play with my new ball in the pool?" Yesterday, Cathy had bought the inflated, bright-colored plastic ball, the size of a volleyball, from a sidewalk vendor on her way home from work.

Cathy felt incredibly weary. She didn't think she could tolerate Angel's incessant "why's" if she tried to keep her in the apartment all day, simply to avoid Darrin. It wasn't fair to Angel, anyway. Darrin was *her* problem. Or rather her feelings for him were the problem.

"We'll see," she murmured.

Angel was rarely satisfied with that answer, and this morning was no exception. "If I drink all my orange juice and eat all my cereal, can I?"

"Maybe."

"*And* pick up all my toys?"

Cathy smiled, in spite of herself. Sometimes she thought Angel would end up as a professional arbitrator. At three, she was already a canny bargainer.

"All right. And don't gulp your food. There's plenty of time."

Angel picked up her glass with both hands and took a swallow of orange juice, then set it down carefully. She smiled benignly at Cathy. "I love you, Mommy."

"I love you, too. A whole bunch." Cathy sprinkled a teaspoon of sugar over each bowl of corn flakes and added milk. Angel began to eat. Cathy closed her eyes and pressed hot fingers to them. The headache was better. She could move now without setting off hammers in her head.

She'd have to go in the pool with Angel, of course. Darrin might come out, but he had to be faced sooner or later. She couldn't go on avoiding him. It was too awkward—impossible, really, since he lived in the same complex. Besides, she didn't think he'd let her get away with it indefinitely.

Why had it never occurred to her that someday, somewhere she might meet a man like Darrin?

"Mommy, aren't you going to eat your cereal?"

She sighed inwardly and, opening her eyes, stared at the soggy flakes in her bowl. She took a few half-hearted bites, noticing that Angel's bowl was empty and she was draining her glass.

Sliding off her chair, Angel said, "I'm going to pick up my toys now. Can I put on my bathing suit then?"

"Yes," Cathy said, "but let's wait for our breakfast to settle a little before we go out."

"'Kay," Angel agreed, if reluctantly, and ran out of the room.

The garbage disposal gobbled the rest of Cathy's cereal, but she lingered over her coffee, wishing that she were an ordinary single parent, like Gwen. But even getting a divorce hadn't been ordinary. When she'd fled to Houston, found Rachel and announced, "I want a divorce,'' she'd thought that part at least would be simple.

"Fine," Rachel had said, sitting Cathy down in her living room with some brandy. While Cathy drank it, Rachel had dealt with Angel, who by that time was walking in her sleep.

When Rachel returned from the guest bedroom, she'd sat down next to Cathy on the couch and said, "Now, start from the beginning."

Cathy had, from the day she'd met Frank until the moment she'd landed on Rachel's doorstep. Rachel interrupted a few times to ask pertinent questions. When Cathy had finished, Rachel had poured more brandy into both their snifters.

"You can really pick 'em," she muttered. "What a mess."

"I want it behind me as soon as possible," Cathy said fiercely. "How quickly can you get me a divorce?"

"I see a few problems with that. In the first place, you have to establish residency in Texas before you can file."

"How long?"

"Six months."

Cathy groaned. "I don't like it, but I guess I can stay here that long."

"You can't file suit as Mary O'Connor," Rachel had said dryly, repeating the name Cathy had used to book her flight to Houston. "You'd have to use your own name and that would go into the record."

Cathy shivered violently. "Couldn't you push it through in a day or two? I mean, if I wait until I establish residency to file, couldn't you get the hearing set for the next day? I could be gone before Frank . . .''

Rachel raised a hand to stop Cathy's spate of words. "That's not how it works, honey. When you file, a notice of the divorce hearing will be sent to Frank's last known address."

"I—I could give the wrong address."

Rachel sighed and set her snifter on the coffee table. "Child, you are such a babe in the woods. The notice would be sent certified mail. The hearing couldn't be held until after the return receipt came back. We can schedule it ahead of time, say a couple of weeks after the notice is mailed, but if there's no receipt, the hearing will be cancelled."

Cathy stared at her incredulously. "Frank would have to sign for it— Oh, no. He'd be in Houston the same day and I'd have to go to the hearing and . . . no, he'd have me followed. He'd find me. . . . I'll go to Mexico. . . ."

Rachel placed her cool fingers over the agitated hands twisting around each other in Cathy's lap. "You could get a divorce there without establishing six-months' residency, but not without a piece of paper showing the other party was aware of the divorce action."

"Oh, God!" Cathy shoved her fingers through her hair in a tearing motion. "What am I going to do? I have to get free of him."

"Let me think for a minute," Rachel mused. "All that's required is the return receipt showing that somebody at Frank's residence signed for the certified letter." She looked at Cathy for a long moment. "You never heard me say what I'm about to say, all right?"

Cathy nodded tiredly.

"Is there anyone in Frank's house you can trust, someone who would sign for the letter and conveniently misplace it for a week or so, until after the hearing? If Frank didn't show up with his attorney to contest the action and get into the matter of Angel's custody, you'd be granted the divorce and custody by default.''

''Rosie,'' Cathy whispered. ''She's the maid who helped me smuggle Angel out of the house. She might be willing to do it, but I hate to put her in jeopardy again. Even if Frank believed the notice was misplaced, he'd be so furious he'd fire her.''

''It's the only way I can think of for you to get a divorce and custody of Angel without Frank finding out about it until it's too late.''

So when the time came, Cathy phoned Rosie. The young Chicano woman had agreed with hardly any hesitation. Rosie had figured out what Frank did for a living long before it finally dawned on Cathy, and she despised the whole business. Mr. Kampion was away, she told Cathy, and nobody knew when he was expected back.

He's out looking for us himself, Cathy had thought as a finger of ice traveled up her spine. As for Rosie, she wanted to leave Frank's employ, anyway, but finding another job was proving difficult. She would wait until the certified letter came. If she'd still not found another job by then, maybe she would say yes to the handsome Chicano who'd been plaguing her to marry him and move with him to New York. One way or the other, she'd be gone before anybody found that envelope.

Still, Cathy had been in a state of terror up to the day of the hearing. But neither Frank nor his attorney had appeared and the hearing was over in minutes. Cathy was granted a divorce and custody of Angel.

They left Houston the next day, as Catherine and Annette Prentiss.

If only she could believe that had been the end of it.

Her musings were interrupted by Angel's voice calling for Cathy to come and tie the straps of her life jacket.

The pool, which few of the residents ever used in the mornings, was not in use when they went out to the terrace. They played in the water for an hour before Angel was tired enough to call it quits. They crawled out of the pool and Cathy handed Angel one of the towels she'd brought. She dried herself with the other, then bent over to wrap it, turban-style, around her wet hair.

When she straightened, Darrin was walking around the pool toward her. Their eyes met and neither looked away until Angel spotted him and ran to meet him, laughing as he swung her up in his arms and deposited her flat on her back on an inflated raft, one of several scattered about the pool area.

When he turned back to Cathy, his white T-shirt and denim cutoffs were wet where Angel had squirmed against him. He didn't seem to mind. "Hi," he said.

Cathy realized that she was smiling and blushing. Perhaps he'd attribute her high color to the fact that she'd been in the sun-splashed pool. "Hello, Darrin."

Angel scrambled up off the raft. "Catch my ball, Darrin."

Wheeling, he snatched the ball out of the air and sent it across the lawn in a high arc that ended in a periwinkle bed. Whooping, Angel ran after it.

"That should keep her busy for a couple of minutes," he said with a devilish grin.

Cathy gave a half laugh, ignoring the fluttery little feeling in her stomach. "You shouldn't have made her like you so much. She'll pester you to death now."

"I don't mind. She's a great kid, but I wanted to be alone with her mother long enough to invite her to dinner tonight."

She tried to pull her gaze from his suddenly grave eyes, but couldn't. The fluttery feeling grew worse. "There's no one to sit with Angel."

"What about Gwen?"

"I'm sure she gets enough of it during the week. Besides, she's seeing someone. I imagine they have plans."

"Then bring Angel with us."

For a moment they stood still, watching each other. The pulse at the base of her throat beat thickly. His gaze raked the length of her flushed, slender form in the one-piece suit that was cut high on each side over her thighs, exposing tantalizing, inverted Vs of bare skin. His fingers curled into his palms at his sides and she wondered if it was because he wanted to touch her as much as she wanted to touch him.

"I got it, Darrin," Angel shrieked, running back across the lawn.

He closed his eyes briefly, as though the sight of Cathy had suddenly become too much for him. "Seven," he said.

And then he was gone.

"Did you buy this car?" Cathy asked. They were driving up a twisty, narrow road to Frenchman's Hill in the old town with Angel between them. It wasn't quite dark yet.

"Do you really think this is my style?" Darrin asked wryly. The American-made car was a nondescript, bottom of the line. "It was the only one available at the rental agency."

"It's not so bad," Cathy said, amused. "But, no, it doesn't seem to fit you. You're more the sports car type."

He flashed her a quick grin. "Hate to disappoint you, but I own a sedan. It costs too much to ship it. I left it with a friend."

"I'm not disappointed. Surprised, maybe."

"Why?"

"I guess I thought a writer would be a little more, uh, daring in his choice of wheels."

He laughed. "Writers buy what they can afford, like everybody else."

"Sensible, too. I have to tell you, you're destroying my image of the writer as a high-flying free spirit."

He glanced at her across Angel's head, one eyebrow cocked rakishly, a smile hovering around his mouth. "The car's red."

She grinned. "Thank goodness. That helps enormously."

Unable to tolerate being ignored by the adults any longer, Angel flounced in the seat and asked, "How long before we get there, Darrin?"

"Half a minute," he told her as they topped the hill. He parked beside the restaurant, once a nineteenth-century manor house. "I'm told the view from up here is spectacular."

Inside the restaurant, the look and feel of casual elegance reigned. They were escorted to a table in one of the two dining rooms that had once been high-ceilinged parlors. The warm glow of candlelight shimmered on softly polished mahogany. A montage of sweeping arches framed a dramatic view of the room and the harbor strung with lights. Someone was playing a piano in another room: "Lara's Theme."

"It's beautiful," Cathy murmured when they were seated.

He watched the candlelight flicker across her lovely face and the simple silk shantung dress that was the color of jade. Brown had called him earlier in the week to report that none of the fingerprints taken from Wenger's condo were Kampion's. Perversely, Darrin had been pleased to hear it, even though it would have meant a tremendous break in the case.

He smiled at Cathy, bemused by his unprofessional reaction to Brown's report. Tonight her only jewelry was a gold neck chain and tiny gold studs at her ears. Hers was the kind of beauty that didn't need to be enhanced by any ornament.

The golden-tanned skin above the dress's scooped neck was flawlessly smooth. The tips of his fingers could almost feel its warm, silky texture. "Yes, it is," he said. "Blindingly beautiful." He held her eyes with his glittering gaze.

She stared at him. His smile was gone and there was no teasing in his eyes, and she knew he wasn't talking about the view. What she saw was longing, and she felt the tug of its seduction. She knew in that moment that she could not live indefinitely without a man to be with, talk to, make her feel like a woman. She wanted this man to make love to her.

Shaken, she welcomed the distraction of the waiter placing a menu in front of her. It was a reprieve from the disturbing direction of her thoughts.

The menu was a mix of French and Italian dishes with a few island specialties and fish, steak and chops. Angel required her attention for several minutes, as she helped her decide what she wanted from the children's menu section. It was long enough for her to recover her composure.

After the waiter had poured two glasses of the white zinfandel Darrin had chosen, and left with their orders, she settled back in her chair. The fingers of her right hand curled around the stem of her glass. "This must have been a lovely house once. It's easy to imagine it as the home of a wealthy plantation owner. He might have been descended from one of the original Danish settlers."

He lifted his glass, looking at her over its rim as he swallowed. The faintly mocking tilt of one corner of his mouth as he set his glass down seemed to say he knew she'd searched for a perfectly safe topic and settled on the house. "He might have been a Dane, but I doubt a house as costly as this one was built from plantation profits. More likely, it was built by a trader. There was a time when Charlotte Amalie was one of the world's richest ports. Ships flying just about every flag on the globe stopped here. Everything from exotic spices to human flesh was bought and sold here."

"Slaves?"

He nodded. "For thirty years, St. Thomas was the biggest slave market in the world."

She shook her head, looking bewildered. "I can't believe a slave trader built an elegant house like this. It's too...too incongruous."

Her bewilderment apparently amused him because a smile hovered around his mouth. "Flesh peddling and good taste aren't necessarily mutually exclusive."

Then even as she watched, his mood seemed to shift. His expression darkened and he gazed down into the wine in his glass. I'd give anything to know what brought that shade down, Cathy thought.

In fact, Darrin was thinking that she, of all people, knew the most despicable men could have impeccable taste in homes and art—and in women—Frank Kampion being a case in point. Evidently a drug trafficker was less offensive to her sensibilities than a slave trader. He looked up at her, frowning. It wasn't possible that she didn't know what her husband did for a living. Was it?

Before he could pursue the question, Angel announced, "We used to live in a *big* house."

For a moment, nobody said anything. He saw the quick, almost imperceptible flare of shock in Cathy's dark blue eyes, noticed that her hands shook as they reached for her glass. Her face paled. She gripped the bowl of her wineglass in both hands, as though the fragile glass could steady her, and drained it.

"Did you really?" Darrin asked, his tone innocent in its blandness. "When was this?"

"I don't remember. It was a long time ago." Angel shrugged, losing interest in the topic. "I like it better here, anyway."

Darrin shot a questioning look at Cathy. Encouraged by the wine, color was returning to her face. "We haven't lived in a house since she was two. I'm surprised she can even remember. But after living in apartments for so long, I guess any house would seem large."

Smooth, Darrin thought, as the waiter approached with their dinner on a tray. Very smooth. If only the meal had been delayed a few more minutes, what might Angel have said next?

To Cathy, the food proved a heaven-sent diversion. It was well past Angel's usual dinnertime, and she began to eat immediately. The remainder of the meal passed without another disturbing incident. Cathy spent most of it worrying about how many other things Angel remembered from when they were with her father. How often did she think of them? And when might she innocently blurt out something far more distressing than the remark about the house?

At length, she realized that, although Darrin and Angel had been chatting amiably, she'd hardly said a word during the entire meal. "I'm a real dud as a dinner companion tonight, I'm afraid," she said.

"You do seem preoccupied."

His eyes imprisoned her. She could feel herself being pulled as strongly as if he had reached across the table and gripped her with his big hands. She resisted. He was a man no woman dare take lightly. Behind those hazel eyes were depths that could swallow you up. They would never release you if you ventured into them. Yet she couldn't deny she was tempted. "I'm sorry."

"It's all right." His eyes smiled at her, scattering her thoughts. "Would you like dessert?"

"I couldn't possibly. And I think I should get Angel to bed."

"I'm not sleepy," Angel protested.

"Oh, yeah?" Darrin teased. "Then how come you need toothpicks to prop up your eyelids?"

She rubbed her eyes, giggling. "There aren't any toothpicks," she said disgustedly.

He tugged on her earlobe. "Must have been a trick of the candlelight." He looked at the check in the small, leather folder left by the waiter, placed some bills inside and laid the folder beside his plate. "Come on, big'n, let's go home."

They hadn't been in the car more than two minutes before Angel was asleep, her head in Cathy's lap. Cathy's fingers combed gently through the child's hair. Darrin maneuvered the car carefully down the narrow, winding street. He didn't take his eyes from the road as he asked quietly, "What are you thinking, Cathy?"

She sent a quick glance in his direction. "You wouldn't be interested."

Darrin narrowed his eyes. "You couldn't be more wrong," he murmured. "Nothing would interest me more than to get inside that beautiful, secretive head of yours."

Wary, she shifted Angel into a more comfortable position. "You'd find my secrets terribly boring."

"Try me."

She stared through the windshield. They had reached the bottom of the hill and were driving along Veterans Drive, the lights of the town reflected in the black water of the bay. "I don't think so," she murmured.

He knew he mustn't press her. He hadn't really expected her to confide in him yet, but he was aware of a sharp disappointment, all the same.

When they reached the apartment complex, he carried Angel inside. Cathy unlocked the door to her apartment and turned back to him. The faint hope he'd had that she would invite him in was dashed when she said, "Thank you for tonight. I'll take Angel now."

He stifled a desire to insist upon carrying the child inside to her bed and shifted Angel's weight to Cathy.

"Thank you again," she said.

"Cathy." His hand brushed her hair, her cheek, and then curled beneath her chin. Leaning forward, he brought his mouth down to hers. Her lips parted immediately and her tongue met his, searching, tasting. Her flavor was sweet and compelling. Greedy, he dove deeper, frustrated at the barrier of Angel's body. He wanted nothing between them. He heard her muffled moan and his thumb felt the sudden race of her pulse at the side of her throat. A dark urgency filled him. It jolted him back. Battling his will into line, he forced his fingers to drop away from the warm and satiny skin of her throat and broke the kiss.

"Even asleep," he muttered thickly, "Angel's a great little chaperone. When are you going to let me see you alone?"

She stared at him, cheeks flushed with passion, eyes dark with it. Her mouth was moist and swollen from his, her lips parted, her breath coming rapidly.

"Darrin." She said his name huskily, and then didn't seem to know what to say next.

"Why are you afraid of me, Cathy?"

For a second, she seemed too bemused to understand. Then she blinked, as though awaking, and color flooded her face. "Oh, Darrin, it's not you. It's—" She wanted him to kiss her again. She was so hungry for a man's love. "Could you come to dinner Thursday night?" She said it all in one breath before she could change her mind.

Thursday was Dawn's birthday. Angel had been plaguing Cathy to be allowed to sleep over at Dawn's that night. She'd always said no before, but now she changed her mind. Gwen was right. She would smother Angel with her overprotectiveness. It was impossible to avoid all risk. Life itself was a risk. The trick was to make sure the risks you took were calculated. Angel would be as safe with Gwen on Thursday night as she would be with Cathy. "I'll cook for you. Could you come at seven?"

The invitation was obviously impulsive, but Darrin didn't question it. Apparently she was moving closer to trusting him. He'd learned not to look gift horses in the mouth. He stepped back before he could touch her again. "Seven is fine. You'd better go in now."

"Good night," she whispered. Turning, she stepped inside and pushed the door closed behind her.

Chapter 8

Eight-thirty p.m. Cathy heard the muted sounds of rich orchestra music coming from the living room: *Beethoven's Fifth*. Darrin had turned on the tape player, the volume low.

She removed the cover from the carrot cake she'd baked that afternoon and took down two dessert plates. Not too surprisingly, her hands were shaking. She gripped the edge of the kitchen cabinet to steady them. She was a nervous wreck. A hundred times between Saturday night and tonight, she had thought of calling Darrin and canceling dinner. Because she knew, when he learned that Angel was sleeping at Gwen's tonight, he'd naturally assume she expected the evening to end with him in her bed.

She took a deep breath and relaxed her grip on the cabinet. Admit it, Cathy, she ordered herself. Hadn't the shivery images of Darrin and her bed merged in her mind Saturday evening, when she'd made the snap de-

cision to let Angel sleep over at Gwen's and then
blurted out the invitation to dinner?

Sighing, she gave rueful mental assent to the question. The thought had been there, along with the be-
wildering jumble of emotions that Darrin's touch
always aroused in her. She had had repeated second
thoughts since then, especially at night, alone in her
bed, when she couldn't sleep.

He'd probably had no trouble sleeping, she thought
in disgust. Whatever implications he had seen in her
invitation, he certainly appeared to be at ease this evening. Obviously *he* wasn't in an emotional whirl.

Alone in the kitchen, she could feel his fingers cup-
ping her chin as they had Saturday night, his thumb
brushing the pulse that beat at the side of her throat.
The taste of his mouth. The press of his body against
hers, that night on the lawn. Desire churned in her tired
body, fueled by the quick, hard kiss he had given her
with the roses when he arrived. She couldn't even remember what they had talked about over dinner. All
she could remember was the deep timbre of his voice
and the intent gaze of those deep-set hazel eyes.

She struggled to calm her rapid heartbeat. She felt
the ache that had sat in her stomach all evening grow
heavier. Coffee, she thought, and grabbed the glass pot
from the automatic coffee maker on the counter. They
would want coffee with dessert. And perhaps a table-
spoon of brandy in each cup. Maybe the brandy would
calm her jitters. She ran cold water into the pot and
poured it in the top of the coffee maker. After adding
grounds, she plugged it in.

She cut two pieces of cake and arranged them on the
plates. Watching the coffee trickle slowly into the pot,
she tried to remember if Darrin used cream or sugar.

She had seen him drink coffee, but she couldn't recall whether he'd added anything to it. But then her brain wasn't working very efficiently tonight.

She walked across the kitchen toward the door leading into the living room, high heels tapping on the tile floor, her full silk skirt whooshing around her legs.

"Darrin, how do you take—" She halted abruptly in the doorway. Stunned and confused by what she saw, she gripped the doorjamb. Shock rendered her momentarily speechless.

Darrin was silently cursing himself. While she was in the kitchen, he'd taken the opportunity to look through the secretary for anything that hadn't been there when he'd searched the apartment. He'd leafed through a pile of mail, which contained nothing but bills and the announcement of a new exercise spa that was opening nearby. When he heard her coming, he'd scrambled to return the mail to the drawer where he'd found it. In doing so, his hand had closed over a small, hard cylinder. Recognizing the shape instantly, he'd pulled out the gun. He was turning it over in his hand when Cathy entered the room.

It was a .22-caliber automatic. It had a chrome barrel and mother-of-pearl grips. He removed the clip and checked the chamber. It was empty.

He stared at it for another moment. With one part of his mind, he was automatically memorizing the serial number, and with the other, he was wondering where it had come from and when. It hadn't been in the apartment when he'd searched it. Had she met someone in St. John, after all? Not Frank Kampion, but one of his goons, who had given her the gun. But why now? Why did she feel she needed a gun, all of a sudden?

Cathy's shock drained away as anger took over. It slowly seeped into her that he had been going through her desk. "What in hell do you think you're doing?" she demanded.

Shaken by his discovery of the gun, Darrin schooled his face to show no emotion. "Where did you get this?"

She saw the hard set of his jaw. His eyes fixed on her were cold and determined. There was nothing apologetic about his expression. He was angry, she realized as her stomach tightened. What was going on? Had she misread the evidence of her own eyes? No, that was impossible. He had been looking through the secretary.

"I think you'd better leave."

He heard the ice in her voice. He laid the gun on the desk and walked to her. "Where did you get it, Cathy?"

Her eyes stayed level on his. "I'm not going to tell you that. I'm not going to tell you anything."

But her voice shook. Darrin thrust his hands in his trousers' pockets. "Do you know how to use it?"

"I asked you to leave." Her voice was stronger now, touched with pain. "I can't throw you out bodily, but I can telephone for help." She tried to step past him, but he blocked her way. The pain was sharp with the sense of betrayal. She lifted her chin and stared at him. "Tell me, Darrin, are you a common sneak thief, or simply nosy?"

"Stop it, Cathy." He looked away first because he couldn't stand the way she looked at him. He began to pace back and forth between her and the desk. He raked his fingers through his hair and shook his head. "You little fool!"

He spun and was striding back to her with the words. She sprang toward him, hand upraised to slap his face. He grabbed her wrist before the contact was made. "Damn you!" she flung at him, her fury matching his own.

Frustrated, he shook her. "Where's the ammunition?"

"In that drawer, in a sack," she spat out. "Don't tell me you missed something."

"Don't you know it's dangerous to keep a gun around where a child can get hold of it?"

"Of course, I know that! It isn't loaded. Now, go, dammit!"

"Shut up and listen to me," he snapped. "I'm not kidding around. I'm going to know where you got that gun before I leave. Believe it."

She had never seen this hard, relentless side of him before. "Something's going on here that you're not telling me," she tossed back. She was confused by his reaction. There was no indication that it was he who was in the wrong, not she. She jerked away from him and stormed to the couch. A headache had started throbbing in her right temple. Sitting down, she rubbed the spot with her fingers. "I got it from Gwen," she said wearily.

"Gwen!" He strode to the couch and stood, staring down at her. She couldn't be lying. It would be too easy to check. "Is it hers?"

"No."

"Then where did she get it?" he asked, straining for patience.

After a thick silence, Cathy said, "She thinks a woman living alone needs a gun—for protection. I didn't ask her for it. She just brought it. I put it in that drawer and I haven't touched it since. I'd forgotten all about it.'' She didn't look at him.

He watched her press fingertips against her temple. ''Great. A .22 is all the protection you need, as long as you aren't attacked by something bigger than a poodle. And you haven't answered my question. Where did Gwen get it?''

She hadn't wanted the gun in the first place. But why was he so angry? If it hadn't been so frightening, she would have laughed. She closed her eyes. The deep bass rhythm of Beethoven's symphony seemed to be inside her head. ''From Jeremy Teller, the man Gwen's been seeing. I didn't ask where he got it. I didn't want to know.''

Her toneless voice worried him more than her anger had. ''Have you ever shot a gun in your life?'' He spoke slowly, deliberately. ''Because if you haven't, there's no way you'd be capable of using it on an intruder. Even if you had a cannon, you'd hesitate and get the thing rammed down your own throat.''

She was growing tired of this. What gave him the right to lecture her? ''You're wrong.'' Her eyes sprang to his face, defiant now. ''If somebody came in here and tried to take Angel, I wouldn't hesitate an instant to empty that gun, and don't tell me that wouldn't stop him. To protect my daughter, I will kill if I have to.''

''You're talking about a hired kidnapper?''

''Yes.''

Oddly, he almost believed her, even though it made no sense. She sounded so fierce that he certainly believed she could shoot an FBI agent if she learned he was on to her. But she wouldn't have invited him to dinner tonight if she suspected him. Yet she *was* frightened of something. How could he get her to level with him? With a frown, he said, "The gun is probably stolen."

Her color drained, and she rose slowly to her feet. It appeared the thought had never occurred to her. "Why do you say that?" she whispered incredulously.

"Did you sign papers?"

She shook her head, but he'd already known the answer. She wouldn't have risked using a false name and using her real name would have been an even bigger risk. "I don't know this Teller, but he's surely not stupid enough to register a gun in his own name and then give it away."

"Gwen said that Jeremy would know how to get a gun. It never even entered my mind..."

She wasn't pretending. How could Frank Kampion's wife be so incredibly naive? It seemed a contradiction in terms. "Well, there won't be any trouble unless I have to use it, and—" she took a deep breath and a hint of color began seeping back into her cheeks "—if I have to, the fact that it's stolen will be the least of my problems."

He was relieved to see her color returning. But the fingers she lifted to massage her temple were trembling. He went to the glass-doored corner cabinet where he'd noticed a small liquor supply. He poured brandy into a snifter and carried it to her. "Drink this."

She accepted the brandy and drank deeply. "For the record," he said, "I am neither a sneak thief nor a snoop."

She looked at him a long moment before speaking. "Then why were you going through my things?"

Darrin lifted his shoulders in a half shrug. "I thought I had a reason. That's all I can tell you."

Frowning, she lifted the brandy again. "You couldn't have been looking for the gun. You didn't know it was there, unless— Did Gwen tell you?"

"No."

She noticed that he didn't say he hadn't known about the gun, only that Gwen hadn't told him. She didn't know what that meant, if anything. But with the brandy soothing the ache in her stomach and the pounding in her head, knowing seemed less important than before. He'd have passed the desk as he crossed the room to the tape player. Perhaps on the way back, he'd taken a look in that drawer out of simple curiosity and was embarrassed to admit it.

"There aren't any dark secrets in the secretary or anywhere else in the apartment," she murmured. "But I still don't like people going through my things."

"I'll remember that." She was going to let it drop, he thought, feeling some of the tension leaving him. It would be easy enough to check on the gun. "I think you should keep the thing locked up, though. Kids have been known to figure out how to load a gun."

He was right, Cathy realized. She'd been careless. Regardless of what else had fueled the relentless anger she'd seen in him, he was concerned for Angel's safety, and hers. And now she understood why she'd decided to peel off yet another of the barriers between them, in spite of the emotional risks she'd never thought she could take. With him she felt safe. "I'll lock it up tonight."

"In your bedroom would be better."

"All right."

He looked down at her, knowing he'd finally succeeded in impressing upon her the dangers involved in having a gun in the house. "If you really think you need protection, hiring somebody to keep an eye on the apartment and on Angel might be a better idea."

"A private detective?" The suggestion seemed to alarm her.

He nodded. "I could check into it for you, find somebody who's reliable." He was thinking that Brown could impersonate a private eye.

She was shaking her head before he finished speaking. "No. I don't want anybody watching me." A shiver passed through her, and he knew better than to pursue the idea.

"Do you still want me to leave?"

"No." A desperate boldness seized her when she thought of his leaving her with the aching need that had taken up permanent residence in the pit of her stomach. "I . . ." Something very like tenderness was stealing into his eyes. She looked away from it. "Please stay."

"Gladly. I thought I was going to miss dessert." He tried for a light tone but didn't quite bring it off.

She had forgotten the cake and coffee. "I don't mean . . ." She moistened her lips. "I wasn't thinking of dessert. Could you . . . would you stay with me afterward . . . I mean tonight."

She looked up at him, soft, vulnerable, scared. The tape player had switched off, and the silence that followed her words was deafening. He heard his heart start to pound in his ears. God in heaven, he wanted her. Use some sense, he ordered himself, but sense was being lost in the thunderous pumping of his blood. He should leave now, at once, before it was too late.

"Cathy, are you sure that's—" Wise. He had started to say *wise*! Like a damned accountant about to advise against an imprudent investment. He could feel himself losing control. Desperate, he raised a hand. To do what? he wondered, and then his fingers curled around her throat and he could feel the wild scramble of her pulse beneath his palm.

Her eyes didn't waver. They darkened with need so staggering that it hit him with the force of a blow. He wanted her with a violence that threatened to erupt with the next heartbeat. "You'll live to regret this," he told her in a dangerously quiet voice.

She could barely make sense of his words over the dull thunder of her heart. But she could see how fiercely he was trying to control his need for her in the rigid stillness of his face. "You accused me of being afraid of you, but you're afraid, too. Of what, Darrin?"

His eyes clouded with the desire that he struggled to keep in check. "Of you," he said thickly, pressing his thumb against her frantic pulse, feeling the throb of it in his own blood. "You scare the hell out of me, lady."

His face blurred before her as her eyes misted with longing. She lifted her arms, feeling as though she moved under water, languid with its resistance. She ran her hands slowly up his back, feeling the hardness of muscle and tension beneath his shirt. With sensitive fingertips, she brushed the back of his neck and the hair that lay smoothly against his head, examining the feel and texture for the first time. She felt his neck muscles stiffen beneath her hand, but there was a barely perceptible shifting of his lower body toward her. She pressed against him.

"Damn... Oh, God." With a groan that was half anger, half surrender, his mouth came down to plunder hers.

She plunged into the mindless whirl of her senses, clinging to him fiercely as he crushed her closer. She welcomed the heedless passion that a single touch of his hand could unleash. She felt it flood through her and moaned deep in her throat. There was no tenderness in the kiss. It was a savaging of mouths, his as well as hers. They were both a little mad, and Cathy didn't shrink from that. She gave it free reign. Let the madness take her to its heart where she had never been.

He jerked her silk shirt from the waistband of her skirt and, thrusting both hands into the neck opening, pulled the two sides apart, not knowing or caring whether the buttons slipped free of their holes or popped off. His hands flowed over her heated skin. Never had he imagined such yielding, silken softness.

She shuddered and tore blindly at his shirt until she had it open and her hands could mold the smooth hardness of his back, the roughness of the mat of chest hair. She was trembling uncontrollably now.

Darrin muttered an oath, frustrated with the clasp of her bra. Somehow he got it off, unclasped or ripped, he didn't know. The single button at the waistband of her skirt came free and the skirt dropped away from her, forming a silk puddle around her feet. The next thing he knew, her panty hose and panties were gone. He had no awareness of how he'd disposed of them.

Her stomach was flat, her thighs slim and strong, and when he ran a hand over them, her body was wracked by a convulsive shudder, instantly followed by another and another. Dimly, he knew he teetered on the edge of a treacherous cliff. He had never meant to go this far. He threw his head back, trying to clear it.

She pressed her open mouth against his throat, murmuring, "Please, please..." Her breasts were a warm, pliant pressure against his chest. Her fragrance filled his nostrils and migrated with a swift dizziness to his brain, like a strong narcotic.

She clutched his hand and brought it back to her stomach, pressed it there. As though with a will of its own, his hand moved lower, found the warm moistness and, within seconds, she reached a cataclysmic peak, gasping and convulsing. She swayed, and he held her to keep her from falling.

Going back now was impossible. He abandoned the tattered shreds of his sanity and swung her into his arms. There was nothing but the throbbing need of his body and the soft pliancy of hers. He tore his clothes off and was in her bed, with no memory of the separate movements that had brought him there.

She writhed beneath him, showering a delirious rain of wet kisses over his face and neck while his hands touched her everywhere, covering her body with their burning imprint. The bedspread and sheets beneath her were hopelessly tangled by the wild abandon of their need for each other. Their bodies were damp with perspiration from the fire in their blood. Their breathing was loud and ragged. His breath shuddered hotly against her skin as his tongue darted into secret, quivering places. He took her to the dark heart of the madness where the wild storm raged.

His tongue traveled down between her breasts and into the hollow of her stomach. Her mind reeled and her nipples hardened with need. He pressed openmouthed, nibbling kisses along the line of her hipbone. Mindlessly, she drove her fingers into his hair, wanting him deep inside her, wanting the battering storm to fling her to the peak again, wanting to feel the exquisite, racking pleasure once more.

His tongue journeyed to her breast where his teeth nibbled hungrily at the swelling flesh, circling first one breast and then the other, moving with agonizing slowness toward the center. She writhed and arched against him until he drew her nipple into his mouth, releasing darting flames of pleasure. His mouth was wet and hot and, as he began to suckle, she cried out.

He'd known she wanted him, that there was passion smoldering beneath the surface, but her wild responsiveness was more than he'd expected. It thrilled him and threatened to drown him in its heat. He struggled to hold back the tide. He wanted to plumb the depths of her passion and his own before he opened the floodgates fully.

He wanted to know every inch of her body before he was through. He wanted to touch it and taste it and bury himself in it. Her skin had a fragrance of its own, a clean, delicate scent that got in his brain and intoxicated him. He could feel her ribs, each one clearly defined. Her waist was incredibly slender, her hips seductively, firmly rounded. While his hands discovered all of this, his mouth left her breasts to seek out other delights. As he moved lower, her breath came harder and faster, shuddering out. Over and over, she murmured his name.

Finally, his tongue sought and found the last secret place, the moist center of her need, and he gave her release after release, his own need held in abeyance by the power of hers.

Cathy wanted the agonizing pleasure to go on and on until she was emptied. Though she was exhausted, her body sang with life. She wanted the final, the best pleasure while her body still throbbed in every pore. She found his lean hips and long, muscled thighs. She found the throbbing need between his legs and whispered, "Now, Darrin, please...."

He moved over her and she lifted to meet him. They came together fiercely, gasping, the shock and power staggering them. The shudders started instantly and raced through them both for what seemed an eternity.

Totally spent, they lay tangled together, gasping for air. The tingling of Cathy's skin left slowly. Her body ached with exhaustion. Her mind wondered and marveled. She had been married, borne a child, but she had never experienced anything like what had happened with Darrin. She knew, without understanding, that she would never experience it with anyone else.

She lay among the tangled bedclothes and listened to the deep, measured breathing that told her he had fallen asleep with his arm thrown across her stomach and her head nestled on his shoulder. She remembered the cake and coffee still sitting on the kitchen counter and smiled.

Then, like hungry beasts who had seen a camp fire and caught the scent of cooking meat, doubts and fears began to creep back into her mind.

Why couldn't she have met Darrin years ago before Frank came into her life? If she had, there would never have been a Frank. But wishing did not make it so. It did not give her freedom. She was divorced, legally free, yet she remained a prisoner in a cell from which there was no way out. Frank would not forgive and forget.

She would never have gotten away from him in the first place if she hadn't spent months laying the groundwork after his refusal to discuss a divorce and custody of Angel. She had finally realized she had to use misdirection and deceit if she ever hoped to get away.

Gradually, she had convinced him that she had decided to stay and make the best of the marriage. She had smiled and said all the things she had said before, only suddenly they almost clogged her throat when she forced them out. But she had forced them, knowing she had to. She had let him use her body and feigned a response while biting the inside of her mouth to keep from crying. She had schooled her mind to center on something else, anything else. Until, at last, he had trusted her enough to go out of town and leave her with Angel on the estate.

Terrified of bringing Frank's wrath on her head, but more terrified of staying, she had carried out the plan she had spent months perfecting. She had given Angel a mild sedative and put her to bed. Then she had dressed for the opera and a party afterward in the city, from which she would not be expected to return until the wee hours of the morning.

While Cathy reported in detail on her plans for the evening to the guard Frank had left in the house, Rosie had carried the sleeping Angel out through the servant's wing and into the garage. Laying Angel on the back floorboard of Cathy's car, she had covered her with a light spread the same color as the car's interior.

Her heart pounding hard enough to explode from her chest, Cathy had handed her mink stole to the guard, lifting her hair while he dropped it around her shoulders. She had waved goodbye and entered the garage through a door off the master suite. As she backed the car down the drive, she saw that the guard had come out on the porch. Trembling with fear, she slowed the car as she passed near one of the yard lights so that he could see she was quite alone. Perspiration was running off her in rivulets beneath her glittery clothes. She flashed the guard a smile and another wave and backed into the road. She drove off, gripping the wheel with white-knuckled hands. As soon as she was well away from the estate, she pulled over and sat for several moments, with the motor running, trying to stop shaking.

She hadn't really believed she'd done it until the plane landed in Houston and there was no one waiting for her at the airport. She had double-crossed Frank, and she knew how harshly Frank dealt with double-crossers. What, she wondered, did he have planned for her if he ever found her?

A chill ran through her and she turned her face into Darrin's neck, pressing close to him. She had made a mess of her life, and now she had dragged Darrin into it. She felt the ache of tears in her throat and drew in several deep gulps of air to keep the tears from spilling out.

Darrin stirred, mumbled in his sleep, and turning on his side, wrapped her in his arms. She wound her arms around him and pressed her cheek against his heart, listening to its slow, steady beat. It made her feel protected.

Slowly her eyes grew heavy. Swaddled in the warmth of his body, sheltered in the strength of his arms, she fell asleep.

Later, Darrin awoke slowly from a deep, deep sleep. He must have been dreaming, but he couldn't remember the dream. In the darkness he could feel the breeze from an open window and see the soft billow of a curtain. But the window was in the wrong place.

He shifted and felt the drowsy movement of a hand along his flank. Gradually, he became aware of where he was, of whose face rested against his chest and whose soft, warm breath brushed his skin.

The memory of the final scene in his evening with Cathy slammed into his mind with a staggering, brilliant clarity. Oh, no. He almost cried out the words. How could he have let it happen? How could his control have vanished so completely? And, dear God, could he prevent its happening again?

He had to.

Gently, he lifted the hand that still rested warmly on his flank. Before he could move it away, Cathy stirred and murmured, "No." Her voice was lazy with sleep.

He stilled as she pulled her hand from his grasp and brushed it down his side. "Mmm," she muttered and ran a light trail of kisses over his chest and up to his shoulder.

"Cathy." His body stiffened with the effort not to respond. He would never be able to think of anything but her while her touch raised ripples along his skin and he inhaled her fragrance and the scent of sex in the tangled sheets. If he was going to find his way out of the hole he had dug for himself—he felt the bottom still giving way beneath him, even now—he had to think.

He shifted his shoulder away from her mouth and turned on his back. She merely lifted her fingers to his face and tilted her head to kiss his jaw. "Don't leave me," she whispered. "I need you to hold me...please."

It took all his strength to resist the gentle press of her body along the length of his side. He wanted nothing more than to crush her to him. "This is crazy. You'll be—"

"I'll be sorry tomorrow," she interrupted, "and maybe you will be, too. But I don't want to think about tomorrow right now." When she turned his face so that her lips could find his mouth, an involuntary shudder ran through him, and he knew she felt it. "I want to make love with you again. I have never wanted anything more." Her teeth nibbled gently at his bottom lip, and his heart surged and battered against his eardrums. She pressed her hand against his chest, where his heart betrayed him. "You want me, too. Do we have to think beyond that tonight?"

She shifted so that she lay atop him and lifted her head above his. Her lips were only an inch from his. He could see the tangled cloud of her hair, the silver shimmer created by the moonlight on the curve of her cheek and chin. He saw the twin flames that glittered in her eyes before he cupped the back of her head and brought her mouth down to his. He was her prisoner again.

Chapter 9

When he awoke, the sky framed in the window facing the foot of the bed was smoky with approaching dawn. He could hear the deep, slow rhythm of her breathing. She had been totally spent—they both had been—after they had made love the second time. She had dropped immediately into the deepest sleep, the kind in which you neither move nor dream.

She lay on her side, one knee bent, one hand curled on the pillow beside her face, the other resting lightly in the palm of his hand. Even in sleep, he had not been able to relinquish contact completely.

He eased his hand from beneath hers and rolled out of bed. The hand he had been holding contracted and then relaxed, and she took two shallow breaths before her breathing returned to the same regular rhythm as before, and she slept on. He followed the trail of his clothes from the bedroom, grabbing each piece as he went. In the living room, he dressed hurriedly, then let himself out and made his way back to his own apartment.

He reached his bedroom, continuing to hold his thoughts at bay. He undressed again, dumped the clothes in the hamper and stepped into the shower, remembering that this wasn't the first time he'd stood there until her lingering scent had finally been driven from his memory by the piney smell of the soap.

A black depression descended on him, and his thoughts refused to remain suspended any longer. Why did this woman affect him so deeply? She had done nothing but lie to him since the day they met. Now, she had a gun. Well, she was afraid of *something* if not for the reason she gave him. He felt a fleeting suspicion that he was being manipulated. Oh, hell, of course he was. What do you expect? he asked himself savagely. You're as guilty of deceit and manipulation as she is. But last night had been neither of these. Last night had been a thing apart. Last night was not supposed to have happened.

Later that day, he called Rainey and gave him the serial number of the gun Cathy had in her apartment. "Call me back when you find out who it's registered to."

"ASAP, right?" Rainey asked.

"You got it."

"Sure, Boyle. It's always a rush job when *you* want the information. Another story when I'm trying to pry something out of you."

Darrin ignored the tone of hard sarcasm. "There's something else I want you to check out for me. See if there was a lawsuit filed for the custody of Angela Kampion anytime during the past three years. Check

Massachusetts, where the grandmother lives, as well as California."

"Dammit, Boyle," Rainey barked. "Don't tell me you're starting to believe her."

"No, but I want to cover every possible angle. The woman's afraid of something."

"Hell, yes, she is. Wouldn't you be a tad apprehensive if you knew a team of Feds was combing the globe in search of you and your old man?"

"Yeah, yeah," Darrin said impatiently. "Do me a favor, Rainey. Humor me. Okay?"

"That's what I spend half my time doing. Call me softhearted. If I weren't, you'd have had your butt kicked back to the boonies long before now." With that, Rainey broke the connection.

Darrin hung up, unruffled by Rainey's parting shot. Softhearted, in a pig's eye. Rainey didn't put up with him out of any tender feelings on his part. Rainey wouldn't know a tender feeling if it hit him in the face. The only reason Rainey would tolerate insubordination from any of the agents who reported to him was that he thought the man was of enough value to the bureau to be worth it. Rainey wanted him in Washington. He also thought Rainey would follow up on the custody matter. Cursing and grumbling all the way, but that was part of the package when you were dealing with Rainey.

Darrin's assessment of the situation was proved correct when Rainey called him back two days later. As usual, he wasted no time on civility. "The gun's registered to a retired bookkeeper named Arthur Pendergast. He's seventy-one-years old and lives in St. Croix. Christiansted. Owned the gun for twelve years. He reported it stolen four months ago with a coin collection worth nearly two hundred thousand. The local police say Pendergast's house had been burgled by a pro. Took nothing but the gun and the collection, which was fully insured, by the way. Nothing else worth taking."

"Did Pendergast need the insurance money?"

"The investigating officer says no. The old man lives modestly on a pension from the company where he worked for thirty-five years. Says Pendergast was inconsolable. He'd been adding to the collection since he was twelve years old. He put the insurance money in a CD, and he still calls the officer every few weeks to ask if the investigation is ongoing. He hasn't touched the money. They've checked. Pendergast says he's keeping it to pay back the insurance company when they recover the coins."

"I hope they do."

Rainey snorted. "Fat chance. That collection is scattered all over the world by now."

"What about the custody suit?"

"A lot of wasted man hours spent on checking that, but I expected it." He couldn't resist adding, "You've wasted my time before." But Darrin knew Rainey hadn't spent a minute on the project. He'd assigned it to an underling. "I even checked our sources again on the woman's parents and Kampion's father," Rainey continued. "All dead and buried. No mistake."

"Very thorough of you, old man."

"There was no custody suit, Boyle," he said with some relish. "Not in California. Not in Massachusetts. Satisfied?"

"Satisfied."

"Now, about the gun—"

"Somebody at the door," Darrin lied quickly. "I'll check in later."

What you might call mixed reviews, Darrin mused as he hung up. The gun had clearly come into Cathy's possession just as she'd said. Gwen Nettleton's boyfriend had contacted somebody who knew where to get stolen firearms. On the other hand, Cathy's lie about the custody battle was now confirmed. Not that he had really doubted it would be. Hoped, maybe, against the evidence and all logic, but never doubted.

Cathy's week had seemed longer than any she could remember. When she'd awakened Friday morning and found herself alone in her bed, she'd expected Darrin to call her later that day. When he hadn't, she'd thought she would hear from him during the week. She was prepared for his call. She knew she had to tell him she couldn't see him again. In her circumstances, it couldn't end any other way and dragging it out would only make it harder, make it hurt more.

She rehearsed how she would tell him, over and over in her mind. But he hadn't called. She hadn't even caught a glimpse of him, though once or twice she'd sensed he saw her from inside his apartment when she came home from work; but she hadn't let herself glance even once toward his kitchen window.

Angel had badgered her all week to help her make brownies for Darrin. Cathy had put her off with one excuse after another, while the passing of each day left her more tense and apprehensive. On two separate occasions, both late at night when she'd been undressing in her bedroom in the dark, she'd felt the tingling at the back of her neck that had been her constant companion in the months after she'd left Frank—the powerful conviction that she was being watched. But when she'd peered for a long time into the darkness from behind a bedroom curtain, she had seen no movement, nothing but the ghostly shadows of shrubs and trees.

Obviously, Darrin had decided he didn't want to see her again. But oddly she needed to see him one more time, long enough to tell him that he'd been right about the regret he'd predicted. She did wish that she could wipe out the disastrous mistake they'd made Thursday night. She would admit that it was as much her fault as his. Probably more so since, in the end, she'd been the aggressor. He had wanted to leave before it was too late, but she had overcome his hesitation.

Only once more, she told herself, and only long enough to say what had to be said. Perhaps then there would be a feeling of completion, of ending, about the relationship. Perhaps then the strain she was under would go away and she would stop imagining that some malevolent presence was stalking her.

Knowing he had to see Cathy again and follow up on the start he'd made at gaining her trust, Darrin procrastinated until late Saturday night, long after Angel would have been put to bed, before going to Cathy's apartment. He'd watched her going and coming from work all week, though she was unaware of it. She had never once looked in the direction of his apartment. He wondered if she had been expecting him to call, wanting him to. Or she might be glad that he hadn't.

His depression still clung to him, the black awareness of a man who has committed himself to a hopeless cause but has too much at stake to turn back. The only way around was through.

He didn't even know what he would say when she opened the door. For a moment, she merely stared at him with a look of resigned acceptance. She wore a white terry robe and wisps of hair curled around her face, still damp from the shower. There were shadows beneath her eyes, dark smudges against pale skin.

"Cathy—"

"You were right."

"You regret it," he said resignedly. "I wish I could say it doesn't matter. I wish I could tell you it won't happen again."

"It can't."

"Why?" He had his own very good reasons why it shouldn't happen again, but he was curious about what reason she could give. He didn't think she would be honest enough to tell him the truth. If only she would.

"You might as well come in," she said tiredly, and added as he stepped inside, "for a few moments."

He watched her go to the corner cabinet and take out a decanter, as though she needed something to do. Her eyes met his in the gilt-framed mirror next to the cabinet for an instant before she looked down. "Sherry?"

"Yes, thanks."

She poured a small amount into two stemmed glasses and offered him one. He drank the sherry in one gulp and set the glass on the coffee table. She sank into a chair and took a sip of her drink before looking up at him. For a moment they were still, watching each other.

Cathy could feel his frustration and the anger that she had given up trying to understand. It probably stemmed from what must seem to him the game she was playing, sending out unmistakable come-on signals and then pushing him away. Indian giving, they had called it in her childhood. In her teen years, she would have been labeled a tease, probably preceded by a crude but descriptive adjective. But she hadn't been that kind of girl at all. She had been shy and unbelievably innocent, which was why Frank had found it so easy to deceive her. Not that any of it mattered now.

He jammed his fists in his pockets. "Why can't it happen again, Cathy?"

"I... Oh, Darrin, my first marriage was such a mistake. I haven't been involved with anyone since...since my husband died." Her voice grew stronger as she gained confidence from his attitude of listening intently. "I don't want to make another mistake. I'm not ready for...for someone like you. Beyond that, my situation, well, I've explained this to you before."

Moving his shoulders in the cotton shirt to ease their tension, he ordered himself to relax. "Tell me again. Spell it out for me."

She set her glass down on the side table, alerted by the deceptive softness of his words. She curled her hands over the arms of the chair. "Angel's grandparents have people looking for us. If they find us, and I can't stop them, they'll take her away from me."

"Kidnap her, you mean," he prompted, "after losing their custody suit—in California, wasn't it?"

She nodded, watching him. Had she ever told him she'd lived in California? She must have.

Before she had time to think about that, he stepped toward her, leaned down and placed his hands next to hers, gripping the arms of the chair.

"Stop lying to me, Cathy." His voice was rough with suppressed anger.

Her chin shot up. "I'm not!"

"There has been no custody suit—" the words spewed out of him against his will, like steam so swollen with heat it had to find an escape valve "—for any child named Prentiss in California in the past three years." In spite of the loss of verbal control, he still had enough restraint not to say Kampion.

She struggled up out of the chair, pushing him away with both hands. "How do you know that?" she cried. It didn't matter that he'd looked for the wrong name; he'd have found nothing if he'd known the right one. What mattered was that he'd been checking out her story in the first place.

Belatedly remembering Angel, she darted a glance toward the hall where a narrow strip of Angel's closed bedroom door was visible. When no sound came from that direction, she spun back to face Darrin, her eyes ablaze with anger.

Cathy had suddenly remembered the strong sense of being watched that she had felt once or twice during the last week. "You hired a private detective, didn't you? After I told you not to. But, then, he wasn't protecting Angel, was he? He was checking up on me." The thought of his going to such lengths infuriated her, but it accounted for her feeling of being watched, and it was more palatable than the thought that someone working for Frank might have tracked her down.

Darrin had used the brief seconds of her distraction to gain more control of himself. "No."

"Then how did you find out?"

"My brother," he improvised, adding a shrug that almost cracked the taut muscles on either side of his neck. He dropped in a few more details to bolster the improvisation. "His wife's uncle is a police officer. He has a contact in some law enforcement agency in California.'' All quite vague, but it seemed to satisfy her. It didn't do a thing to lessen her anger, though.

"The unmitigated gall!'' she hissed, flinging the drying tendrils of hair out of her eyes. "How could you be so underhanded?''

"Call me whatever you want. I had to know. You should give up lying, Cathy. You aren't very good at it.''

She stared at him, her eyes narrowed and calculating. Brushing past him, she walked to the door leading into the hall and closed it, putting two doors and the hallway between them and Angel.

She spun around and walked the length of the living room to stand at a window, where the light from the table lamp barely reached, her back to him. The slats in the blinds were partially open, leaving narrow lines of exposed glass with blackness on the other side. The window was on the long side of A-wing, facing a strip of lawn and a retaining wall bordered by shrubs. Darrin wondered if she'd been looking out that window earlier and, if so, what she'd been looking for.

"Turn out the lamp, please,'' she murmured, still with her back to him, and adding, as he did so, "I don't want to be seen, if there's anyone out there.'' Now the room was gray and dim, the only interior light coming from the kitchen. It was dark enough to see a few stars winking in the narrow strips of windowpane.

"So,'' she murmured. All the anger was gone from her voice. She sounded merely stoical. Perhaps she wasn't used to lying and she was relieved that he finally knew a fraction of the truth. She turned to face him. "You know I've been lying to you, and you've had the satisfaction of telling me so to my face. Why are you still here?''

He walked to her. "Because it's obvious that you're afraid. Who do you think might be out there, watching you?"

"No one, I expect. I've been wrong before—several times." She tried for a smile. "Maybe I have a guilty conscience. Like Poe's murderer who kept hearing his victim's heart beating beneath his floor."

He lifted the back of his hand to her face and ran his knuckles over the line of her cheekbone. He wondered if she knew how great his need was to touch her. "You're not a criminal. Talk to me, Cathy."

"I can't, not—I can't."

He heard the hesitation and knew she had almost said "not yet," as though she needed to be more sure of him before she could confide in him. The possibility was there that she would confide in him eventually, although it could be that he only wanted to believe that.

"Whatever it is, it's wearing you down. Your eyes are shadowed. You aren't getting enough rest. I should go and let you sleep," he said, his voice thick with emotion, but his lips were already lowering to find hers.

The brush of his mouth on hers was gentle and comforting. Cathy lifted her arms to circle his neck and leaned against him, helpless in the face of his tenderness to do anything else. His fingertips flowed over her jawline and her cheek, probing gently along the edge of the bone above one eye, as though he wanted to memorize her features. She sighed and parted her lips in answer to the gentle questing of his mouth, and sank into the kiss.

Their lovemaking last Thursday night, even the second time when they'd been languid with sleep, had been touched by a driving, primitive need that had to be sated. But this slow, seeking tenderness was equally impossible to resist.

Beneath his thumb, the pulse below her jawline was a deep, steady beat of desire. Tonight, whatever she was afraid of, he wanted to free her from the fear and satisfy all her needs. Nothing else mattered in that moment. Feeling the swell of emotions in his chest— some unfamiliar, others well-known—he loosened the tie belt at her waist and drew the robe down off her shoulders. Together they sank to the carpeted floor, the robe spread open beneath them.

Cathy watched with dark, intense eyes, as he sat beside her, his gaze sliding over her as he undressed. She smiled at him, feeling cherished, and brushed her fingers over his shoulder, down his chest and along his thigh. She realized it was crazy to imagine that she could make love with him for one night and then send him away.

His fingers enclosed hers and he leaned over her to bring his mouth to her parted lips once more. She felt as though she were floating on a quiet sea, the waves rippling gently beneath her and all around her. His kisses were soft, his murmured words, tender. She had not imagined him capable of such gentle endearments.

He released her hand and brushed her hair away from her face and combed through it slowly, as though to savor the feel of the strands sliding through his fingers. He brought his hand to her lips, tracing their outline with indulgent care. She kissed the tips of his fingers and felt a quiver pass through her. With trembling hands, she touched his face, feeling the faint rasp of beard on his cheeks and chin. Framing his face in her hands, she searched his intense eyes, feeling their power. She brought his mouth down to hers, heard his incoherent murmur, felt his heated flesh as he slid, full-length, atop her.

Oh, I love you, she thought, as they began to touch and taste each other, seeking, lingering, seeking again. There was heated flesh and pounding hearts and labored breathing, but encompassing all of that was a peaceful tenderness. They did not speak often, and then only in whispered murmurs of pleasure. Each knew, without words, how to meet the needs of the other.

Darrin had known passion with other women. He had been told that he was an exciting, considerate lover. But no woman before Cathy had ever drawn from him this deep and calming need to give until he had given all he was capable of. He knew the name of that need, but did not form the word in his mind.

In the gloomy half darkness, he gave to her what he had hoarded and protected from the invasion of other women. His hands and eyes and mouth made adoring sacrifices to the shrine of her body. Flushed with the heat of their blood, languid with desire, Cathy lay quietly, every trace of doubt and inhibition washed away in a sea of pleasure and sensation.

Wanting to give him everything, she captured his mouth as it hovered over her lips and, nudging gently, turned on her side, facing him. She wet his lips with the tip of her tongue, tracing their shape. She tasted the corners of his mouth, then slid inside to savor the sweet flavors there. Her hands slid beneath his arms and glided down long, hard muscles to mold to the small of his back, fingers splayed down over his hips. Her need fueled higher, she moaned and melted against the length of him.

The waves, no longer lapping gently, leaped with the rising winds of escalating passion. His need matched her own, and slow savoring began to give way to hot, greedy urgency. His mouth traveled over her, devouring. Her body hummed a wild song of joy. His name was a moan deep in her throat, as she wrapped her limbs around him and rolled on top of him.

She lifted to receive him and, with the wet, hungry joining, her name was torn from his lips as they crushed hers. The ascent was swift and wild and desperate. They went over together, his mouth muffling her groans of delirium.

After a while, there was perfect stillness. Coming back to herself, Cathy listened to the quiet, remembering her daughter, knowing that she hadn't awakened. What would she had done if Angel had? How reckless to make love in the living room while her daughter slept in the bedroom down the hall. But prudence, along with everything else, had been driven from her mind as it was filled with Darrin.

Drifting in a haze of weariness, she lay beneath him. His breath was warm against her throat, but soft now and regular. She barely had enough strength to lift a hand and rest it against his hair.

He rolled her gently off him and lifted his head to look at her. Her eyes were glazed and heavy-lidded. "You need to rest now."

"Now I'll be able to," she murmured.

Rising, he lifted her and carried her to her bed. He tucked the sheet around her and kissed her gently as her eyes drifted closed. Her hair fanned out, dry now. She was so small, he thought, so slender and fragile to be able to deal with a man like Frank Kampion. How had she gotten involved with him? Did she love him? He shook the questions from his mind.

"I'll turn out the kitchen light and lock the door behind me when I leave."

A smile drifted over her lips and she murmured an incoherent syllable. Then she was asleep.

Chapter 10

He loved her.

It was the worst thing that could have happened to Darrin, and what was he going to do about it? What *could* he do?

Love interfered with his objectivity, clouded his judgment. If Rainey found out he was bedding Kampion's wife... If Cathy found out who he really was...

Throwing off the sheet, Darrin crawled out of bed and began to dress in running shorts and shoes. It was early yet, and he could get in a run before the morning heated up. When he came back, he'd call Cathy and ask if he could take her and Angel to breakfast. He'd stay close to them until this case was closed, and then...

Then he'd go back to Washington and never see them again. Cathy wouldn't want to see him anyway when she found out he'd been using her. He'd get out of Cathy's life and get her out of his head.

* * *

Sunday brunch at Charlotte Amalie's largest hotel was a lavish meal served buffet-style, and popular with the natives as well as tourists. Waffles and hot maple syrup. Scrambled eggs. Canadian bacon and sausage links. Hot blueberry muffins and puffy biscuits and whipped butter. Apple butter and strawberry preserves and peach jam. Platters of attractively arranged melon slices surrounding bite-sized pieces of fresh island fruits: mango, pineapple, banana, genip, soursop, mammee apple, plantain, guava and breadfruit.

Darrin, Cathy and Angel carried their plates to an outside table on the hotel's awning-shaded, flagstone terrace.

"Darrin," Angel announced, as Cathy tucked a napkin beneath her chin, "Mommy promised we could make you brownies after my nap. You can help if you want to."

"I'll see if I can make it," Darrin said, looking to Cathy for her reaction. After lunch, they were going to Coral World, St. Thomas's underwater observation tower and marine park.

Cathy's face was still pale, but the shadows beneath her eyes weren't as pronounced as before. "Don't commit yourself too hastily. By then, you may have had more than enough fun for one day," she said, leaving open the option not to invite him to the apartment later. But her smile was soft, her eyes glowing with warmth as she said it.

"You look as though you could do with a nap later, too," he told her.

"I can't sleep in the daytime."

She was wearing a simple, sleeveless cotton dress with a scooped neck that exposed the deep hollows above her collarbone. She must have lost at least five pounds since he arrived in Charlotte Amalie, five pounds she hadn't needed to lose. It worried him that she didn't take better care of herself. "You should get some pills."

"I don't take pills." She'd never been very interested in the "recreational" drugs some of her college friends has used, and since she'd learned what Frank's "business" traded in, she'd developed an abhorrence for drugs of any kind. She couldn't even watch the television exposés on the nation's growing illegal drug problems without feeling sick to her stomach.

Darrin frowned, aware that he'd unwittingly struck a nerve. Her movements seemed jerky as she cut Angel's Canadian bacon into bite-size pieces. "I wasn't suggesting anything strong. Maybe something over-the-counter."

Having dealt with Angel's meat, she sat back and reached for her coffee. She sent Darrin a look that said, Drop it. She wouldn't tell him that she didn't dare take anything that might make her sleep through a break-in at her apartment. She wouldn't tell him of the nightmare that had wakened her at 3:00 a.m., of the sound of stealthy footsteps that might have been a part of the dream, or of the clammy fear that they had, instead, been just outside her bedroom window. She wouldn't tell him that she'd been afraid to go back to sleep after that. She wouldn't tell him that she had reached for him, had needed his arms around her and discovered he'd gone.

Stabbing a piece of pineapple with her fork, she looked across the terrace at the gazebo where glass doors stood open to the tropic air. "There are hardly any empty tables left."

Darrin followed her gaze for a moment, then brought his eyes back to Cathy. "I've heard they do a booming business, especially on Sundays and Fridays. They serve their Grand Buffet Sunday evenings and a West Indian buffet on Friday nights."

"I wish you would bring us here every Sunday, Darrin," Angel said.

"My daughter doesn't know the meaning of tact." Uncomfortably aware that Darrin had been studying her quite intently, she feigned a sudden interest in her scrambled eggs.

"Three-years-olds aren't supposed to," he said. "It's one of their more endearing qualities."

Angel gave the adults a puzzled look. "What's tact?"

"It's like good manners, sweetheart," Cathy said. "I'll explain it to you thoroughly when we get home."

"Okay," Angel said with a shrug and busied herself smearing butter and jam on her biscuit.

"Gwen says the aquariums at Coral World are wonderful. Bright-colored tropical fish, some so unique you'd never see them anywhere else. Fluorescent coral, stingrays, giant eel . . . and the view from the observation tower is breathtaking."

He cut off her nervous rush of words by laying his hand over hers as she reached for her water glass. Her skin was too cold for this warm, tropical morning. He tightened his grip, wanting to give her his warmth. "Cathy, let me take you home after brunch so you can lie down, even if you can't sleep. I'll take Angel to Coral World."

She pulled her hand away. "I'm not an invalid."

He saw he'd irritated her. Almost everything he'd said since he'd picked them up had hit a nerve, all of which seemed to be very close to her surface today. She was feeling defensive, but he wasn't sure why. "I didn't even suggest that," he said evenly, "but you may end up one if you don't take better care of yourself."

"I managed somehow for twenty-eight years before I met you," she said, keeping her voice low with some effort. Who was she upset with, really, Darrin or herself? The fact was, she hadn't managed her life even adequately well.

Because she wouldn't confide in him, Darrin felt frustrated and helpless. He wanted to get her alone and shake the truth out of her. Since that was impossible, he said carelessly, "Whatever you say. It's your life." A tight knot had settled at the back of his throat, and he reached for his coffee to wash it down.

"Yes, it is."

Angel had stopped eating and looked worried. "Mommy, are you mad at Darrin?"

Cathy's unfocused anger seeped out of her as she became aware of Angel's alarm. "No, honey." She forced a smile.

"Maybe you woke up on the wrong side of the bed this morning," Angel said seriously. Cathy had suggested the same to her daughter many times, when she was cranky after a nap.

"That must be it," Cathy said, managing a real smile this time. "I'm sorry, Darrin," she murmured. He's not trying to run your life, she reminded herself, he's concerned about you. The sleepless nights and the nightmare weren't his fault. None of the disasters that have befallen you since the day you met Frank Kampion have anything to do with him. All Darrin was guilty of was being the man she'd fallen in love with against her will. Taking a deep breath, she added, "Perhaps I will let you and Angel go to Coral World without me. And I'd like it if you could come over this evening and help us make brownies."

"Good," he said, feeling himself relax. But the next instant, despair crept in. God, what was he going to do about Cathy? She was clearly under stress. And she seemed so vulnerable. He wondered how much she could take before she broke. If he succeeded in putting Frank Kampion behind bars, exposed him to the world as one of the top men in America's drug trafficking underworld, could she stand up under that?

They finished brunch and drove back to the apartment, where Cathy promised to lie down. When Angel had run ahead of him down the hall, Cathy grabbed his arm and said quietly, "Don't let her out of your sight, please. Keep her close to you."

He called for Angel to wait for him at the end of the hall and held Cathy for a moment, laying a cheek on her hair. "Don't worry. I'll put her on a leash, if I have to."

She chuckled tiredly at his effort to cheer her, imagining Angel's outrage, and the noise, if anyone ever tried a thing like that. What she was really asking him for was the reassurance that everything was going to turn out all right, and that he couldn't give. He dreaded the moment when she discovered that, far from making things turn out right for her and Angel, he was the one who was going to bring them the worst agony they'd ever known.

"Cathy, forget about Angel while we're gone." He tilted her chin and looked into her eyes. He saw weariness there, but he also saw dependence and growing trust. "I'll take good care of her. And of you, if you'll let me." For a while, at least, he hoped she would let him do that for her. Then his lips found hers and lingered for a moment. "Turn off your phone," he murmured, "and put a Do Not Disturb sign on the door. If it's still there when we get back, I'll take Angel to my place until you call."

She leaned against him for another moment, drawing from his strength. Darrin didn't know how desperately she needed to be cared for, protected. But she knew, in the end, she might have to face what she feared alone and do whatever she had to do to protect Angel. She straightened her shoulders and smiled at him.

"I know Angel will be safe with you. Just don't let her cajole you into buying one of those elaborate aquariums and a dozen fish. I'd end up cleaning the thing."

Relieved to see her rallying, he answered the smile. "How about one goldfish and a small bowl?"

"That she can handle on her own," she agreed.

Cathy actually managed to sleep for a couple of hours, without dreaming, though she awoke with a nagging headache. Fortunately a single nonaspirin headache tablet took care of it, and she was feeling refreshed by the time Darrin and Angel returned. Darrin was carrying a fishbowl and fish food. Angel proudly displayed a small goldfish in a plastic bag filled with water.

"His name is Spot," Angel announced.

The fish had no spots that Cathy could see. Her eyes met Darrin's and he lifted his shoulders as though to say, Don't ask me where she got it. "Perfect," Cathy said, returning his smile. He, she thought, is very nearly perfect, too. Angel was coming to love him as much as she did. Where was it all going to end? she wondered. She thought there was a good chance that both she and Angel were going to have their hearts broken.

She decided not to borrow any more trouble, remembering one of her father's favorite sayings: "Time enough tomorrow to worry about tomorrow's problems."

Darrin left shortly, saying he had a few things to do. He'd be back after Angel's nap. Cathy knew he wanted to give her more time alone, as well.

Later, the three of them made brownies. Actually, Angel insisted on stirring the ingredients, with a little help from Darrin, buttering the baking dish and pouring the batter into the dish. By the time they got the brownies in the oven, they all had batter on their hands and arms. They licked it off, laughing like three children.

Then Darrin ran water into the sink and added so much dishwashing detergent, suds puffed up over the top of the sink. He scooped up a handful and flipped them at Angel and Cathy. Not to be outdone, Angel and Cathy pelted him with two handfuls. When the dishes were washed, they had to mop the kitchen floor.

By the time Darrin went home, Cathy had laughed so hard her stomach hurt. She hadn't laughed like that in years. Oh, it had felt good. It made her realize how grim she'd been lately, how seldom she and Angel laughed together over something silly. Darrin was so good for them that she had to caution herself not to grow too dependent on him.

Later in the week, she phoned to invite him to a party Gwen and Jeremy were having. "Gwen says I have to bring a man," she told him.

"Give Gwen my thanks."

"I know women ask men for dates all the time these days, but I can't help it, I feel brazen."

"I like you brazen," he murmured. "If you must know, I like you any way at all."

Even as a tingle ran up her arms, Cathy laughed. "Jeremy's chartered a boat, a crew and caterers. The works. We're going to anchor off an uninhabited island and have a moonlight feast."

"Jeremy really knows how to throw a party."

"Well, he *is* in the hotel business."

"What about Angel?"

"Gwen's regular baby-sitter is going to spend the night at her place. I'm sending Angel over there." Not without a few qualms, either. It was the first time in a year that she'd entrusted Angel to anyone but Gwen, Darrin or Rachel Ord's mother the few times she had to go somewhere alone while in Houston.

She'd interviewed Gwen's baby-sitter, a stout, spunky widow in her sixties, and given her the story about Angel's grandparents to impress her with the necessity for caution. Gwen had already filled her in, it seemed, and the baby-sitter assured Cathy that Angel would be perfectly safe with her. She never opened the door to strangers. Once she had called the police on a particularly persistent magazine salesman who was giving her his pitch through the closed door.

"Sounds great," Darrin said. "At the risk of revealing how easy I am, I have to say I'm already counting the hours."

"So am I," she admitted.

"Easy or counting the hours?"

She laughed. It was one of the things she found so endearing in him: he made her laugh. "Maybe both."

The boat was a sailing yacht named *Lucky Lady*. The crew members went about their tasks unobtrusively, well seasoned to crewing charters of partying guests. Liquor flowed and trays of hors d'oeuvres were emptied during the half hour sail through the star-spangled night to the island.

The guests seemed to be mostly friends and business acquaintances of Jeremy Teller, though a few were Gwen's friends. They were a friendly, boisterous group, becoming more so as the drinks added up.

Darrin allowed himself two bourbon and waters, not wanting to dull the edge of his alertness. He watched Jeremy Teller moving among his guests without seeming to. Teller was a stocky, deeply bronzed, handsome man in his early forties. He had a cheerful, outgoing personality that must serve him well in the hotel business. Darrin didn't really think Teller knew anything about Cathy or him or that he had any connection to Kampion. He didn't think the man was involved in serious criminal activity, even if he had bought a stolen gun from a fence. But Darrin remained alert for anything suspicious. Teller had greeted Darrin and Cathy when they came on board and Gwen introduced them. Since then, he hadn't appeared to pay any particular attention to them.

On Darrin's request, Rainey had told the St. Croix police that the woman presently in possession of the gun was on the fringe of an ongoing FBI investigation, and they didn't want anybody making waves. He hadn't named Cathy, but had identified Teller as the intermediary between the fence and the woman. The police had agreed to wait until Rainey gave them the go-ahead before questioning Teller.

Cathy, sitting beside him on a padded bench built into the boat, was chatting with a friendly, sixtyish couple on the other side of her. She was lovely in a slim, white, floor-length caftan banded with wide lace insets. She'd pinned a white gardenia in her hair, and the flower's sweet smell mingled headily in Darrin's nostrils with the briny scent of the sea. She seemed more relaxed than at any time since Darrin had known her, but he noticed she'd turned down more alcohol after a single drink.

She turned to him, placing a casual hand on his knee. "The Demeurs have retired in St. Croix," she said.

Darrin hadn't really been listening to the conversation. He brought his mind back and closed his hand over Cathy's. What *was* Demeurs's first name? They'd been introduced only minutes ago. The wife was Polly, and the man was . . . Willis, that was it. "Did you live in Texas before, Willis?"

"Recognized my drawl, did you?" Demeurs boomed. He was happy, and his fleshy face was flushed. He'd had four whiskeys in the time he'd been sitting beside Cathy. Probably had a couple before he came on board, just to prime the pump, Darrin thought. "Yeah, we're from Houston. I was in the oil business. Sold all my leases right before the oil glut. Got out in the nick of time. Put all the money in municipal bonds." His gaze wandered to a passing crew member. "Hey, sonny, bring me another whiskey and branch water, will ya?"

Polly touched his arm and said hesitantly, "Willy, don't you think you've had enough for now?"

He shrugged off her hand. "Hell, don't tell me when I've had enough. This is a party."

Polly said nothing else, but she watched disapprovingly as he downed another drink and bragged about how much money he'd made in the oil business. Fortunately, a few minutes later, the crew laid anchor. Teller climbed up on a bench and yelled above the din, "Listen up, campers. Dinner will be ready in an hour. Till then, I'll leave you to your own devices while Gwen and I take a dip and otherwise entertain ourselves."

A couple of bawdy remarks were shouted over the general laughter. Darrin grabbed Cathy's hand and pulled her to her feet. "Come on," he whispered in her ear, "let's make our escape."

He led her through the crowd, down the gangplank and up the moonlit beach, running until the yacht and the other guests were out of sight and earshot.

"Stop," Cathy panted at last. "I'm winded." She flopped down on the sand at the edge of the water, pulling him down with her. She leaned back, bracing herself with her hands behind her, gulping air. "Ahh . . . that's better." She tipped her head back to look at the stars.

Her face glowed in the wash of silver moonlight. Leaning over, he cupped the back of her head and planted a kiss on her damp brow. "Do you think Willis and Polly are following us?"

He drew her into his arms, and she settled against him. "Willis would drop dead if he tried. That man is a heart attack looking for a place to happen." She rested her head on his shoulder and looked up at him.

"Maybe all the others will stay close to the yacht, and we can be alone."

He lowered his head and let his lips play over hers. "An hour isn't nearly enough time," he murmured.

She smiled and traced his upper lip with the tip of her tongue. Then she drew back and touched the scar above his mouth. "How did you get this?"

"A cleat landed in my face in a high school football game."

"Oh, I'm sorry." She kissed the scar before moving down to taste his mouth. "Maybe we could miss the boat and stay here," she murmured. "What do you think?"

He cupped her face, looking deep into her eyes. "I'd like nothing better."

Love coursed through her in a swift flood. She wrapped her arms around his neck and forced back the words, found other, safer words. "They'd come searching for us."

"Then we'd better waste no time," he murmured and brought his mouth down to nibble on her ear. "We left our bathing suits on the boat." He tasted the soft, sensitive spot on the curve of her shoulder.

"Mmm-hmm. What a shame."

He slipped the caftan's straps down over her shoulders to expose her breasts. "Why are you wearing a bra?" he grumbled dealing deftly with the clasp.

"Because I'm modest." She chuckled, then drew in a breath as he cupped her naked breast.

"I like women who are modest," he muttered, "with everyone but me."

She laughed, a low sound of pleasure, as his fingers brought a nipple to hardness. "It's a bit late for modesty where you're concerned."

He tongued the taut nipple. She tasted of some heady perfume. He thought he heard her moan, low and husky, before she pulled away and got to her feet so that she could shrug the rest of the way out of the caftan. Then she kicked away her sandals and peeled off her silk panties, looking down at him with a soft, secretive smile. Her skin was like marble in the moonlight, except that it was warm and pulsing with life and need.

As he got to his feet, she laughed and ran into the water. He undressed in record time and waded in after her. She was floating on her back, kicking her feet, languid and moving beyond his reach. "It's so lovely here," she sighed. "Look, Darrin, there's a shooting star. Quick, make a wish."

"I'd rather make my wish come true," he growled. With a few powerful strokes, he reached her and hauled her back to shallower water where he could stand. Throwing her head back, she wrapped her arms and legs around him and laughed softly. "You make me laugh. I like that about you."

Her buttocks fit into the palms of his hands. The pressure of her wet breasts and the grip of her thighs ignited a sudden urgency in him, a flash of fire. "Only that?" he inquired as he flicked his tongue over her throat.

"I could probably think of another thing or two, if I tried very hard," she said, breathless now because his mouth was making hungry forays over her face and neck.

He felt a torrent of passion shudder through her. "Uh-huh...go on. What else do you like about me?"

"I...can't...think...." Her mouth followed his, claimed it frantically.

Nor could he think. Within moments, he was too deep in the feel and taste of her to be aware of anything else. Incomprehensible fragments of thoughts, musky, salty tastes, frantic movements of her hands on his body. Groaning, he shifted her and thrust into her. He plunged into a sultry, liquid world of pure sensation. It started with his possessing her, and was somehow transformed into her possessing him. He couldn't stop it. His very self flowed from him and into her.

Slick flesh slid over slick flesh. Wet mouths, tasting of the salty sea, plundered. Desire ignited their blood until they were shaking and raw from the searing. She clung to him and let herself fall free, soaring with him to the crest, as he drove into her fast and hard. Convulsions ripped through them, fast at first, then slowing as they floated down.

Her head dropped to his shoulder as she melted against him. His arms locked around her, and he cherished her, never wanting to release her. How would he ever be able to let her go?

She lay still, but he could feel the beat of her heart against his chest and hear the gentle lap of the water. He carried her to the beach. She let her legs drift down until her feet touched the sand, but he continued to hold her, pressing her face into the crook of his neck, his palm against her wet hair.

"Cathy."

She lifted her face to look up at him. Her eyes were huge and glistening. He thought his love must be nakedly revealed in his face. He couldn't speak, and he couldn't look away.

After a moment, she kissed him gently and pulled away. She began to dress quickly, pulling the caftan over her wet hair and picking up her sandals, letting them dangle by the straps from the fingers on one hand. "Come, let's walk," she said, sounding quite grave all at once. "I have something to tell you."

After he'd dressed, they walked farther down the beach, carrying their shoes, fingers entwined between them. "Cathy—"

"No, don't say anything," she said quietly. "First, listen to what I have to tell you." She had not thought she'd ever be able to tell him, ever dare to tell him. Not nearly everything. Perhaps the time would never come when she could tell him all of it. But she knew now— the knowledge had been growing in her all day—that she could not lie to him any longer. She had to give him a piece of the truth and, later...well, she wouldn't think about that now.

Even with the decision made, she wasn't sure for a moment how to start. And then she thought, start with the lies that have come from your own lips. The other, unuttered lies could wait a while longer.

She took a deep breath. "My husband isn't dead." She felt the sudden stiffening of his body and the tightening of his fingers around hers, but she didn't turn her head to look at him. She stared down at her bare, sand-soled feet and kept walking. "I lied to you. I'm not a widow. I'm divorced."

He didn't respond for what seemed a long time. She wished she could know what he was thinking and feeling, if he would be able to forgive, if not understand, her deceit. When he did speak, it was without intonation, almost as if he didn't comprehend the word. "Divorced."

She darted a quick look at him. Strands of wet hair were stuck to his forehead, and she had to resist the impulse to smooth them back. His moon-bathed face had changed. It was closed and impenetrable now. "Before Angel and I came to St. Thomas, we were in Houston. An old friend—my college roommate—practices law there. We had to stay long enough to establish residency and then I got the divorce, and we came here."

Darrin was trying to assimilate what she'd said, trying to fit it into some understandable pattern. Of all the things he'd expected her to say, that she was divorced was not among them. Was it another lie? And if so, why was she changing her story now? As long as she was going to lie, posing as a widow was as good a story as any. What she was doing was deepening his confusion. He wondered fleetingly if that was her intention.

When she couldn't stand his silence any longer, she asked, "What are you thinking?"

He stopped abruptly and faced her. "I guess I'm wondering why you said you were a widow in the first place."

"To keep people from asking questions about my marriage and what caused the divorce, I suppose. I can't talk about that." He had let go of her hand, and she wished he hadn't.

"So," he said grimly, "have there been other lies, as well? What about the wicked grandparents who want to take Angel away from you?"

He sounded so cold. But she'd known the risk she was taking when she told him, and she'd had to do it. She was in love with him, and it was no longer a matter of keeping up the pose until he was gone. Whether he went or stayed, she had to tell him as much of the truth as she could. "Angel has only one living grandparent. My husband's mother, who took little notice of

Angel while I was married to her son. She was too busy with her parties, not to mention her cosmetic surgeon, her fitness trainer, her hairdresser and her dress designer. She resented me for making her a grandmother, and preferred to pretend it hadn't happened. She's the last person in the world who'd want to take custody of Angel."

He uttered a hard, brittle laugh. "I didn't give you enough credit, Cathy. I really believed you thought somebody was after Angel. I thought you were scared stiff. You're good, I'll give you that."

"Don't," she said quietly. "Don't hate me until you've heard me out. I am scared. I've been terrified for a year now, and sometimes—" She had to stop and swallow the lump in her throat. "Sometimes I think it will never end. People *are* looking for Angel and me. My husband told me once that if I ever left him, he'd take Angel and I'd never see her again. He—he doesn't make idle threats, believe me. He's a vengeful man."

Her words were low, but they rang with conviction. Yet there was so much she wasn't telling him. How could he trust her completely when everything was so mixed-up with his feelings for her? He couldn't separate his professional objectivity from his very subjective emotions. He slid his hands into his pockets, not knowing what else to do with them.

"I'm sorry," she said softly. "I lied to you and I don't know if you can forgive me. I only know that I couldn't go on lying, not after—" she turned away so that he wouldn't see the tears that had sprung to her eyes "—not any longer."

What did it mean, this sudden passion for the truth—some of it, anyway—he wondered. And how would she react if she knew of the lies he'd told? He was, after all, in no position to play the injured party.

The shrill sound of a whistle came from the yacht's direction. That would be Teller, calling them all to dinner. He cupped his hand over the curve of her shoulder and turned her to face him. "We'll discuss it later. We'd better go back now before they send out a search party."

She didn't reply, but neither did she seem to mind when he put his arm around her as they walked back to the yacht.

Chapter 11

But they did not talk about it later. When he tried, as the yacht got underway again, she said she'd told him all he needed to know. She couldn't talk about her ex-husband, she said, or her marriage. It was still too close, too painful for her.

She was quiet on the yacht going back. He had found a dark corner and sat with his arms around her and her head on his shoulder. After a few stabs at conversation, he let it go. Though she was silent, he knew she wasn't sleeping; she was thinking. He wished he knew *what* she was thinking, how she was feeling.

What Cathy was feeling was despair. She loved him, though love did not seem a big enough word for what happened inside her every time she was with him or even thought about him, which, lately, was most of the time. Loving him merely enmeshed her deeper in the fearful web of the life she'd lived since leaving San Francisco. To salve her own conscience, she'd told him part of the truth and brought him further into the web with her.

Having gone so far, she might as well have told him who her ex-husband really was. She tried to convince herself that not telling him was a way of protecting him. She was very much afraid that, when Darrin did learn all the truth, she would be forever tarnished in his eyes, and he'd leave her.

How could she make him understand why, having married Frank, she'd stayed in the marriage for four years? Would he believe she'd remained ignorant of so much for so long? There had been times in Houston when she'd suspected even her old friend Rachel had had doubts, times when she'd caught Rachel studying her with puzzled eyes, as though wondering if any woman could really be that impervious to what went on around her. Certainly Rachel wouldn't have been. Nor Gwen, she supposed. But then they hadn't been swept off their feet by Frank Kampion at the age of twenty-two.

No, she couldn't risk telling Darrin any more of the truth—not yet.

They picked up Angel at Gwen's and Darrin carried her, still asleep, to Cathy's apartment and put her to bed. Cathy mixed nightcaps and they drank them on the darkened terrace. He half reclined in a patio chaise longue, with Cathy leaning back against him, his chin resting on top of her head.

He waited until they'd finished the drinks to bring up the subject of her ex-husband again. "What went wrong, Cathy?"

She knew what he meant, since she'd been thinking of little else since she'd told him about the divorce, wishing half the time that she'd said nothing and the other half that she had the courage to finish what she'd started and tell him the rest. Obviously, he'd been thinking about her revelation, too. Probably still puzzling over why she'd felt she had to lie to him. It really didn't make any sense unless you knew it all.

"A lot of things," she murmured finally, "but I guess that's true with every marriage that breaks up. It doesn't happen overnight. It takes a while for things to add up until the total is more than you can live with." In her case, it had taken three long years, she thought unhappily, and then it had all exploded into her conscious mind at once. But the worst time had been the last year, after she knew, while she waited and played her part until she could get out with Angel.

"What things?"

She stirred in his arms. "Please don't keep on at me, Darrin," she whispered.

"You brought it up," he said gently. "You said you'd lied, but you balked at explaining why. I'm trying to understand why it was easier to say it was the grandparents who are after Angel, instead of your ex-husband. I need to know why, Cathy."

She sat up and turned to look at him. "No, it's better if you don't know. I shouldn't have told you as much as I did. It's not your problem."

He held her face in his hands. "If it's your problem, it's mine," he said huskily. "Don't you know that?"

She pressed her fingers lightly against his lips. "Shh. You don't know what you're saying."

Frustrated, he said, "If you—"

"Shh," she said again and smothered the rest of the words with her mouth.

It had never been like this for her. Each time they were together, she was stunned by the uniqueness, the wonder of it. And when they touched, kissed, the wonder was consumed by a rush of passion and she lost herself. Needed to lose herself.

How quickly he could take her back to the dark, pulsing center of a world that was all-consuming emotion and body-wracking sensation. Her lips, her fingertips, her skin became sensitive to the slightest nuance of touch. It was as though her nerves were suddenly stripped of any protective covering, left exposed to quiver and hum as his fingers and mouth played over her body.

He began to whisper in her ear. He told her how beautiful she was, how soft her skin felt, how much he needed her. She murmured that he made her feel all liquid pleasure inside, that she had never wanted anyone so much.

He shifted her beneath him and took her slowly, feeling the soft shivers that pulsed through her, savoring the taste of her face and throat. He kept his mind on her feelings, her needs, keeping the rhythm easy, letting the pleasure build slowly.

"Darrin—" Her voice was thready and breathless, as though she could barely form the word. "Say you forgive me—for lying to you."

"Yes . . . I forgive you, love." He had never before used such an endearment. In that moment, at least, he would have forgiven her anything. Would she forgive him anything?

His voice, labored and unsteady, filled her with warmth that pushed her toward the ultimate ecstasy. She struggled to form words as she climbed higher. "No one ever made me feel this way before . . . only you, Darrin."

"It's the same . . . for me."

She sought and found his lips, and his mouth took her cry as he increased the tempo and drove her quickly to the peak. He would always need her, he thought as he felt the convulsions start. Always. And then he could think no more.

They hadn't even taken the time to undress. When he had the strength to move, he sat up, pulling up his trousers, which were down around his ankles. Smoothing her caftan down over her legs, he drew her up and into his arms. She lay against him quietly for a second and then suddenly sat straight up.

"What is it?"

"I thought I heard something." She rubbed her arms as though she felt a chill. "Let's go inside. I feel too exposed out here."

He followed her into the apartment. He had heard nothing. "Get some sleep," he told her. He kissed her gently, held her quietly for a moment and then drew away from her.

She wrapped her arms around his waist. "You don't have to go."

"You won't sleep if I stay." Reluctantly, he removed her arms and went to the door. "I'll call you tomorrow." Before his resolve weakened, he let himself out and walked determinedly back to his apartment. There, he thought about their time alone on the beach, the things she'd told him.

Divorced. It was the last thing he'd expected her to say. If it was true, it changed everything. Maybe they'd been wasting their time, searching for Cathy. Or maybe Kampion really would try to take revenge on her, in which case she needed to be protected, not used.

But was it true?

He started to call Rainey, then decided he didn't want to hear Rainey's sarcasm tonight. Instead, he dialed Brown's home phone number. The young agent answered sleepily after the third ring.

"Sorry to wake you, Brown, but I need your help."

"Sure." The agreement was automatic. It was followed by a pause, while Brown tried to figure out where he was and who was on the phone. "Boyle," he said finally. "Just a minute, let me turn on a light. Okay. What can I do for you?"

"Do you have a weekend number for one of our men in Houston?"

"I have the bureau phone directory in my desk at the office."

"Tomorrow morning will be soon enough. I want you to ask them to check Houston court records. See if a judgment of divorce was granted Mrs. K. sometime during the past year."

"Divorce!"

"Don't ask me to explain," Darrin said sharply. It seemed that he could entertain a doubt about Cathy's story in a dark corner of his mind, but he wouldn't tolerate it from anyone else.

"Okay."

Darrin's harsh tone softened. His confused emotions weren't Brown's fault. "Sorry to ask you to go down to the office on Sunday, but it's important. Maybe we'll get all this kind of information in a single computer bank one of these days."

"No problem, only—" It was clear he still wanted to ask a question about this odd middle-of-the-night request. He managed to hold back the words. "All right. I'll get on it first thing tomorrow."

"Call me back as soon as you know, and thanks, Brown."

Darrin wanted desperately to believe that Cathy really had divorced Kampion. But if he'd learned anything in his years with the bureau it was that you could never wholly trust anybody involved in an investigation. It could get you killed. He had to know one way or the other if there had been a divorce. For the record, and for himself.

He switched off the living room light. He found his way to the bedroom in the dark and stood at a window, looking out at the shadows of trees and a low, night-lighted building half a block away.

Thinking of how Cathy had seemed frightened to stay on the terrace after they made love, he opened a window and listened intently. He heard nothing but the locust-sounding hum of some night insect and, after several moments, a dog barking a good distance away.

If there had been a divorce, Kampion had probably been given visitation rights with his daughter. But Cathy didn't want him to see Angel at all. She seemed convinced that if Kampion ever got his hands on the child, she wouldn't get her back. Maybe he hadn't wanted the divorce. Vengeful, she had called him, and she'd lived with the man long enough to know.

But it had been a year now since she'd left San Francisco—left her husband, according to Cathy. Yet she seemed to think he'd keep paying men to look for her indefinitely. Maybe she was right. And maybe she was just scaring herself.

If one of Kampion's men was watching the apartment, why didn't he act? It was possible that the opportunity to snatch Angel hadn't presented itself yet, but that didn't seem likely. Cathy and Gwen kept a close eye on the child, but if someone was determined, there was usually a way.

Cathy had admitted that she often felt watched, but in a year's time no one had ever actually tried to take Angel or even tried to break into the apartment. She was paranoid on the subject. When Cathy wasn't in his sight, where he could touch her, it was easier to keep things in perspective. He was dealing with a very overworked imagination here.

He knew he wouldn't sleep if he went to bed, so he decided to take a stroll on the grounds. He didn't expect to run into anyone near Cathy's apartment, but, after hesitating a moment, he tucked his gun into the waistband of his trousers. It made him feel a bit foolish.

He walked in the shadows close to the outer perimeter of the grounds, away from the complex's nightlights and the yellow glow from the few apartments where the occupants were still up. Maybe they were victims of insomnia, too.

When his eyes adjusted to the darkness, he scanned the shrubbery close to the building for a shadow that seemed out of place or a movement. He detected nothing unusual and, as the hulking length of A-wing came into view, he was glad to see all of Cathy's windows dark. He hoped she was sleeping and not lying in the dark, listening for suspicious sounds.

His rubber-soled shoes made soft, whispering noises in the thick grass. He stopped a few times to fade deeper into the shadows and listen. No sound, no movement disturbed the still night.

He rounded the front of the building and stopped one last time, in the line of trees outside B-wing, having almost finished one complete circle of the building. He could hear the low murmur of a television from one of the apartments. He rubbed a hand over the back of his neck, wishing the tension concentrated there would leave. Maybe one more circuit would do it, and then he'd go to bed.

As he stepped between two trees to continue his walk he heard a faint noise behind him. Automatically he reached for the butt of his gun and half turned. But he was too late. He heard a grunt and was grabbed in a deadlock grip from behind.

"Drop it, cowboy." The voice was deep and sounded winded. The man holding Darrin crushed back against him smelled of sweat and garlic. "Toss it away from you."

"I can't toss it. You've got my arms in a vise."

There was a lengthy silence, while the man thought it over. Darrin suspected no one had ever described his attacker as rapier-witted. He hoped he wasn't misjudging the man. Finally, the man released Darrin's right arm, immediately pressing something cold against the front of Darrin's throat. "That's a knife you feel on your windpipe," he grunted, "so don't try to be cute."

Darrin swung his arm out, letting the gun drop as close as he dared. "What do you want with me?"

A mocking chuckle rumbled in the man's throat. "You got it wrong, mister. I ask the questions, you answer. How come you're stumbling around in the dark with a gun?"

"I thought I heard somebody outside my apartment, and I came to check."

"Sure 'nough?" he said sarcastically. The knife pressed fractionally harder against Darrin's throat. The blunt side of the blade touched his skin, but in a split second it could be flipped over. "Wait a minute, you're not—" He stopped, then took another tack. "What's the woman to you?"

Cathy hadn't imagined it, then. This strong-arm tough had been watching her, watching them. It didn't have to mean he was looking to snatch Angel. Maybe he was a bodyguard hired by Kampion to protect his wife and daughter. "What woman?"

"Don't act any dumber than you have to. You know who I mean. Emily. What's she to you?"

"I don't know any Emily."

The knife pressed harder, almost cutting off his air. "I'm warning you, chum."

His fingers clawed futilely at the knife blade. "If you mean the woman I was with tonight," he gasped, "her name is Cathy. Cathy Prentiss." He sucked air loudly as the pressure on his throat eased. He had to try something, while it was still the blunt edge of the knife he was dealing with. If he could bring one hand up far enough to grab the man's wrist and kick backward at the same time...

"You're a regular comedian. Her name's Emily. She dyed her hair, but it's Emily Kampion, all right. You tryin' to tell me you don't know that?"

Darrin eased his right hand up slowly and shifted his weight to his left foot. "I've never heard that name in my life. Why are you interested in her?"

"Oops, you forgot again. I ask the questions, remember. Don't you think you're mighty friendly with the lady not to know her name?"

"I told you, it's Cathy."

"You're dead meat, sucker," the man snarled. "Her old man's gonna make you disappear."

He sounded more like a bodyguard than a kidnapper. Darrin pushed the thought aside to be dealt with later. "She's not married."

"Har-har! Now, I'm gonna take a peek at your wallet, see who you are. Just stand there like a good citizen and— Hey, what—!"

In a single swift movement, Darrin lifted his knee and kicked backward with all his might, at the same time clamping his fingers around the man's thick wrist to keep him from turning the knife over. His foot connected solidly with a kneecap.

His attacker howled a curse. Feeling the man's grip on his left arm relax, Darrin wrenched free and grabbed the arm holding the knife with both hands. Bending his knees and heaving, he threw the man over his shoulder. He landed flat on his back and his breath left his lungs with a loud, whooshing sound. Just like in the self-defense films they showed the new recruits at the academy.

Darrin slammed his foot down on the hand that still held the knife. His attacker was too busy trying to breathe and get his hand free of Darrin's foot to keep a grip on the knife. Darrin grabbed it. It was a switchblade. He retracted the blade and dropped it in his trouser pocket. He found his gun just as his assailant was struggling to his feet, cursing and accusing Darrin of crushing his kneecap.

"Stop yelling," Darrin ordered. "If it was crushed, you couldn't stand up."

The man swayed back and forth like a drunk. He was big—six feet and well over two hundred pounds. There was just enough light from a yard lamp for Darrin to see the squashed nose, the thick eyebrows drawing together and the square jaw working convulsively.

He knew the man was thinking of jumping him; he could read it in his face. He braced himself and when the lummox lunged, Darrin stepped to one side and brought the butt of his gun down on the head that had been aimed at his stomach. The man dropped like a stone.

Darrin watched the sprawled form for several moments. It didn't move. Like a felled ox, he thought. Sighing, he grabbed the man's arms and somehow dragged the deadweight over his shoulder. He staggered back to his apartment, hoping nobody had heard the ruckus, wondering what he'd say if somebody came to investigate. Anything but the truth, he decided. He couldn't blow his cover now.

But he saw no one. Panting, he unlocked his door and dragged his unconscious burden inside. After binding the man's hands and feet with strips ripped from a sheet, he dialed Brown's number again.

"You might as well give it up for tonight," Darrin said when Brown's sleep-muffled voice answered. "This time it can't wait till tomorrow."

He had to go through it twice before Brown was awake enough to take it in. "Do you think he's working for Kampion?" Brown asked.

"That's what I want you to find out."

"I'll have to bring in the local police," Brown said. "It's their jurisdiction. If we try to go around them, they'll retaliate by being uncooperative the next time I need a favor. Besides, we don't have any place to lock this guy up while we check him out."

"Do it," Darrin said, "but don't mention Kampion."

While he waited for Brown and the police to come, Darrin looked through his prisoner's pockets. The ID in his wallet said he was Wayne Leroy Vector. Darrin didn't know the name, but it could be a false ID. He found nothing else of interest and returned the wallet to a back pocket.

By the time Brown and two police officers arrived, the prisoner had regained consciousness. He groaned and cursed at first, then clammed up and wouldn't respond to questions. The officers handcuffed him and took him away.

Brown stayed behind long enough to say, "I phoned Houston before I called the local police. Said the divorce check was urgent, couldn't wait till Monday. The man I spoke to promised to go down to the office and get on it." Then Brown left for the police station.

Knowing there would be no sleep for him tonight, Darrin waited. Brown would call as soon as there was any word, either on "Vector" or from Houston.

He made a pot of coffee and drank most of it while pacing the apartment restlessly like a caged beast. The pieces of his investigation were shifting at last. He could feel them moving toward a central point, coming together.

Vector, if that was his name, would talk. Eventually. They might have to bring in a team of interrogators from Washington after the local police had their shot at the man on the assault charge. But Darrin would give it a try first. In the end, the locals would probably be asked to drop their investigation, for if Vector had any functioning brain cells at all, he'd demand immunity from all charges in exchange for his information. Brown could come up with some nonexplanation for his friends in the police department. At this point, Vector was small potatoes. Kampion was the prize. Cathy's husband—or ex-husband. Angel's father....

He heated the last of the coffee in the pot and drank it, standing in his kitchen as the sun came up. His stomach ached with tension and too much coffee. He wondered what the day would bring.

He took out the photographs of Cathy and stared at them for a while, then dropped them back in his attaché case with his gun. Before he knew finally what the day held, he longed to see Cathy. And he was afraid to see her. Stupid fool, he told himself.

Brown's call came at eight-thirty. "I'm still at the police station," he said. "Been bugging the arresting officers all night. I'm lucky they haven't booted me out of here. But civil service has its privileges, right?"

Impatient, Darrin growled, "Get on with it."

"The guy's Wayne Leroy Vector, all right. Idiot didn't even bother to get a fake ID."

Darrin had no time for extraneous commentary. "What do we know about him?"

"He's a suspected professional hit man. Prime suspect in a couple of shootings, but they never got the proof."

"Any connection to Kampion?"

"Yep." Brown was almost gloating. "Washington says he's known to have done a job for The Man from time to time."

Darrin felt a rush of adrenaline. "Has he told you anything?"

"Not yet. To quote him, expletives deleted, he won't talk to 'no pigs in no chicken squat town on no Podunk island.' Wants to talk to somebody important, somebody from Washington with the authority to make a deal. When he started up about Washington, I had to tell the officers we think Vector has some information relevant to one of our ongoing investigations.''

As good a nonexplanation as any, Darrin thought.

''That wasn't exactly a shock to them,'' Brown went on, chuckling, ''since I'm the one who called them to go after Vector, and I've been hovering over their shoulders all night. They'll cooperate. Guess you'll have to come down here. The police already figured out you're one of ours, anyway.''

''I'm on the way.''

''Wait!'' Brown said before Darrin could hang up. ''Don't you want to hear the word from Houston? I called them right before I called you. They'd been trying to reach me at home.''

''Go ahead.''

''Emily Cathleen Kampion was granted an uncontested divorce from Francis Hillyer Kampion on April 16, this year.'' Brown sounded as though he was reading from a script. Even though Darrin thought he was prepared for them, Brown's words hit him like a brass-knuckled fist in the stomach. They removed any justification whatsoever for the way he'd deceived Cathy. She hadn't cheated on her husband. The lies she had told had been to protect her daughter. His lies had no such noble motivation behind them. She would never forgive him.

''Mrs. Kampion,'' Brown was saying, ''was granted full custody of Angela Lynn, daughter of the aforesaid Emily and Francis Kampion. There was no countersuit. Kampion didn't show up for the hearing.''

''He'd have been crazy to. Naturally, he assumed we'd have men there to greet him. Since I've heard nothing about it, I guess we didn't.''

"Right. Nobody in the Houston office knew anything about the divorce until I asked them to check it out. Giant slipup there."

"Yeah. Did Kampion's lawyer show?"

"No. I guess The Man was afraid if he filed any kind of suit, there'd be a paper trail leading right back to him."

That explained why Cathy had been given full custody, but not why she'd been so sure Kampion would change his mind and send somebody after Angel. But she'd been right. If Darrin hadn't stumbled on Vector when he did, it would have been only a matter of days, perhaps hours, before Angel disappeared. Had Cathy's disappearance been on the agenda, too? Vector was a suspected hit man. A sickening knot formed in Darrin's stomach at the thought of what could have happened.

"I have to hand it to you, Boyle," Brown said with sincerity. "She had to trust you a lot to tell you about the divorce. How'd you manage it?"

By sleeping with her and then betraying her, Darrin thought grimly. "I'll be there in fifteen minutes," he said and hung up.

Chapter 12

A police officer unlocked the steel door to the interrogation room and Darrin went in alone. Vector greeted him with a sneer. "If it ain't the man himself." He sat at a gray metal table in a box of a room painted an institutional green, cement floor and all. Dirty disposable coffee cups littered the table. "About time you got here. The coffee in this place is dog vomit.'

Vector leaned back in his chair as Darrin sat down facing him across the table. "You don't seem surprised to see me," Darrin observed.

"Shoulda known when I caught you sneaking around with that gun, Boyle. But I just got to town. I was getting the lay of the land when I ran into you."

"And tried to cut my throat."

He frowned and touched the back of his head gingerly. "I wouldn't have done it. I got no quarrel with the government. You didn't have to hit me so damn hard. Pig."

Darrin shrugged. "You've got thirty pounds on me, and you don't seem to know when you're whipped. I'll bet you were a fighter. In the ring, I mean."

Vector's frown was replaced by a half smile. He fingered his squashed nose. "Long enough to get my schnoz broke three times. I had the muscle and the size, but not the footwork for it. Too slow."

"Pity. But then you found another professional route for your killer instinct."

The grin faltered. The front legs of Vector's chair hit the floor with a bang. The eyes narrowed, grew flinty. "What you insinuating, flatfoot?"

Darrin leaned forward, stared hard into the steely eyes. "Let's cut to the chase, Vector. We both know you kill people for a living."

Vector half rose out of his chair, snarling, "I ain't taking this crap."

"Sit down," Darrin ordered.

Vector stared at him uncertainly for a long moment, then flung himself back into his chair. "If you got proof I killed somebody, charge me and you can talk to my lawyer. If not, shut the hell up."

"We'll leave that for another time. At present, you've been arrested on assault with intent to murder charges. You could be here a long time. You may even get to like St. Thomas."

"Why'd I want to murder you?" Vector snorted. "You can't con a con man, Boyle. You wouldn't be here if you didn't want to deal."

"Maybe, but first I have to be sure I'm not getting the short end of the stick. What do you have to offer in trade?"

"The name of the man I'm working for. And if that gets beyond this room, I'll swear I never said it."

Darrin pretended to consider that a moment, then said carelessly, "Trouble is, Vector, we already know who you're working for. Frank Kampion hired you to kidnap his daughter and murder his wife."

Vector shoved his chair back. "That's it, pig. I didn't come here to murder nobody and I ain't never gonna say I did."

"Suppose you tell me why you did come, then."

Vector glowered at him, thinking it through, trying to figure if it was a trick question. Thinking wasn't his strong suit, so it took a while. Finally, he said, "I was supposed to snatch the kid. That's all."

"Not your regular line of work."

Vector scowled, shrugging.

"If Kampion wanted the child, why didn't he file for partial custody?"

Vector lifted his big shoulders. "Hey, the man don't confide in me. I never even laid eyes on him. One of his errand boys looked me up. From what he said, Kampion didn't even know he was divorced until it was too late. He was sort of moving around at the time. His man said something about a certified letter getting misplaced by some nerd maid. They found it after the maid quit and left town."

"When did you arrive in St. Thomas?"

"Day before yesterday."

"We can check that."

"Check all you want. I was getting paid enough not to rush the job, so I was taking my time, learning her routine. Mrs Kampion's. I didn't want to have to hurt her if I could help it."

"What a compassionate guy."

"It's the truth! I ain't into violence for the sake of violence."

"No, you're into it for money."

Vector folded his beefy arms and looked at the ceiling.

"How'd you find her?"

Vector lowered his gaze and gave him a stupid grin, enjoying himself. "I was told. It was you, Sherlock." He laughed and slapped the table. "That's right. You led Kampion right to her."

"I don't believe you. I've been here for weeks, and you say you arrived day before yesterday."

"Hey, man, believe it or not. Your choice. All I know is somebody gave Kampion the word."

Somebody who worked for the bureau? It had to be, Darrin thought grimly. Somebody not close to the case if they only learned of his arrival in St. Thomas recently. Maybe it was the same person who tipped Kampion that they were about to arrest him, making it possible for him to slip through their fingers. When he left the police station, he'd warn Rainey. He schooled his face to show no reaction.

"Does Kampion know you found Emily?"

"I wasn't really sure myself until today. I have pictures but the hair threw me off. I never had a chance to report back."

Darrin hoped he was telling the truth. Now, for the big question. "We know Kampion has gone into hiding. South America, right?"

"You got me. I told you he don't confide in me."

"The man who contacted you—"

"What are you, crazy? If I let that slip, he's gone." Vector made a slashing motion across his throat. "Hell, nobody tells that numbskull anything. He's a muscle-man. He ain't supposed to know nothing important.''

Darrin sat silent for several moments, thinking. Vector had told him nothing very helpful. It appeared he knew nothing. Well, they'd let him cool his heels for a few days and see.

"So, do we have a deal?"

Darrin stood. "We'll talk again later." He shut the door on Vector's sputtering accusation that he was being double-crossed. "Tell it to the ACLU," Darrin muttered as he walked down the hall.

Brown was waiting for him in the common room. "I want Mrs. Kampion and the child under surveillance twenty-four hours a day," Darrin said, "starting now. And I don't want them to know they're being watched. I don't want them to know anything at this point."

"What'd he tell you?" Brown asked.

"Vector was hired to kidnap the child, maybe murder the woman, though he says not. He claims he wasn't able to report back that he'd found them, but we can't risk it. Besides, it's only a matter of time until they realize something happened to Vector and send somebody else."

Brown nodded and took notes.

"Can you get the police to hold him for a while? I want to talk to him again. And we don't want him out where he can report back to Kampion."

"Sure. It won't be hard to find a way to hold him legally. He did pull a knife on you."

"I'm going home now," Darrin said, "and try to get some sleep."

Darrin's sleep was tortured by dreams. In one of them, Cathy accused him of treachery to her and

Angel. She said he was despicable, he had no heart. She said she never wanted to see him again. Her beautiful blue eyes were filled with hate.

When he awoke in midafternoon, the bed was a tangle of bedclothes. He must have thrashed about for hours. He didn't feel rested; he felt sluggish, as though he'd been drugged.

A hot shower, a sandwich and ice cream helped, but they didn't take away the heavy load of anxiety that weighed on him. How long could he keep Cathy in the dark? Did he have a right not to tell her that Kampion knew where she and Angel were living?

He told himself the less she knew, the better for her. If she learned Kampion had sent a hit man to St. Thomas, she'd panic and run again. At least here, she would be under guard.

He called Brown and was assured that the best security men on the island would be protecting Cathy and Angel—two men when they were separated—at all times. Brown asked Darrin to contact Rainey and get authorization to pay the guards from bureau funds. Their wages could amount to a tidy sum, depending on how long they stayed on the assignment.

When Darrin had got back from the police station, he'd decided against contacting Rainey immediately about the possibility of a snitch in the Washington office. Instead he'd dropped, fully clothed, into bed. Now he broke a near ironclad rule by calling Rainey at home. Darrin filled him in on the divorce and the events of the past twenty-four hours.

After much grumbling and cursing, which Darrin had expected, Rainey agreed to put through the authorization for the money. Then Rainey said, "Maybe there is something to those stories about your charm,

after all. You're real cozy with the little lady, eh?"
When Darrin didn't reply, Rainey went on musingly,
"So she's hiding from Kampion, not us. What do you
know?"

"I tried to tell you she was scared stiff," Darrin bit
out. "And not of us. She doesn't know we're looking
for her husband. She thinks Kampion will try to get the
child, at the very least, and probably have her killed in
the bargain. Maybe it's time to think of taking them
out of here, stashing them in a safe house."

"Uh-uh. No way. For our purposes, it doesn't matter who she's hiding from. She's still the cheese in our
rat trap."

"You're all heart, Rainey."

Rainey laughed, coughed, laughed again. "You stay
put and keep your lip buttoned. Kampion will send
somebody else, and maybe he'll know more than Vector."

Darrin didn't like the relish in Rainey's tone. Anger
rose like bile in his throat. "I think there's a leak at
your end," he said. "Vector said somebody told Kampion the agent on his case was in St. Thomas. He figured I'd tracked his wife and daughter here, since
obviously I wasn't on his trail."

"What!" Rainey sounded as though he were chok-
ing. Darrin wished he would. "Who the hell was it?"

"That's all I know, but I'd suggest you do a little
surveillance of your own."

"Hell and damnation! I'll find out. Heads will roll,
believe me."

"I'll get back to you later," Darrin said shortly and
disconnected. Dropping into a chair, he held his head
in his hands.

God, what a mess he'd made of this investigation. What would be best for Cathy and Angel now? He had his orders, but he'd disobey them and hang the consequences if he thought they'd be safer somewhere else. He'd have to tell Cathy why... He'd have to tell her everything.

Don't let a guilty conscience make you go off half-cocked, he told himself. As things stood, he was in control of the situation. Moving them wouldn't make Kampion change his agenda. He'd find them again eventually, and Cathy wouldn't be free of fear for a minute in the meantime. The only thing that would ensure Cathy's and Angel's safety was Kampion's arrest and imprisonment.

For now, he had to keep up the charade. He had to spend as much time with Cathy and Angel as he could. Even though the bureau had provided security, his presence would give them added protection. He'd feel like a total heel, but he'd just have to live with that.

He phoned her at seven that evening. "Can I come over?" he asked.

"This isn't a good time," she said hesitantly. "Angel and I are just having dinner. I had to work late."

She sounded distant, and she'd had all those excuses on the tip of her tongue. What was going on? "I want to see you. Need to see you."

Silence, followed by a weary sigh. "All right. I suppose we should talk."

Talk about what? Darrin's heart thudded dully in his ears. If she'd found out who he was... No. If she had, she'd react with outrage, not withdrawal.

"Wait until eight-thirty," she said. "It'll give me time to put Angel to bed."

Later, when he knocked on her door, she asked him to identify himself, made him say it twice, before she unbolted and unlocked the door and released the night chain. He noticed the .22 automatic lying on a lamp table.

She saw him glance at the gun. "I didn't get it out until Angel was asleep. I'll put it back in the bedroom later."

She looked beat. Far more wrung out than could be accounted for by working overtime. She hadn't touched him as he came in, and there was wariness in her eyes. He went to her and grasped her shoulders. Her scent flooded his senses. Instant desire roughened his voice.

"What the hell is going on?"

Fear had her trembling. "I saw a man," she managed. "He was outside the gallery when I left work. He had binoculars, but I thought he was a tourist."

He tensed but schooled his voice to casualness. "I'm sure that's what he was."

She gave him an odd, unhappy look. "No. Later I saw him outside this building. I looked out my bedroom window and he was back in a corner of the grounds, leaning against a tree."

Kampion couldn't have sent another hit man so quickly. Great. One of the "best security men on the island" had let himself get made the first day. "Honey," he said gently, "he's probably a resident here, or the guest of one."

"Then why was he hanging around the art gallery?" she hissed as anger began to take over. It suddenly seeped into her that he had never taken her fear completely seriously. Mixed with her anger was the awareness that he was close enough to kiss her. Her breasts brushed his chest. Swallowing, she wrenched from his grasp and walked across the room, putting the sofa between them. "I asked you not to hire a private detective to watch me. Swear to me that you haven't.''

"I swear, Cathy.''

Her shoulders sagged. "Then it's worse than that.''

He said soothingly, "Maybe he's an art lover who happens to be staying with somebody in this apartment building.''

"He never came inside the gallery. And stop treating me like an hysterical woman!" She braced herself against the sofa's back, trying to pretend that she hadn't felt a momentary rush of desire when he touched her. She watched him rake his fingers through his hair, frustrated and uncertain. Welcome to the club, she thought grimly.

"I don't think you're hysterical. I'm sorry if I've given you that impression. But, Cathy, you have to admit you've been under a lot of pressure for a long time.''

Oh, no, he wasn't going to turn this around on her. "I want to ask you a question, Darrin, and I want a straight answer.''

"Shoot,'' he countered.

"Interesting choice of words,'' she murmured, glancing at the .22. He didn't smile. Well, it was a bad joke, and only half a joke, at that. "You haven't said anything about your book for quite a while.''

He stared at her, trying to figure out where she was going. She'd said she wanted to ask a question and then taken a detour, as though the question were difficult for her to utter. Or perhaps it was his answer that she feared. "I've been blocked. It's happened before. It'll go away.''

His eyes fixed on hers were expressionless. She dug her fingernails into the sofa's upholstery. No more side roads, she told herself. "How did you know I used to live in California?"

For some reason, she had been thinking about it that afternoon at the gallery, going back over their times together, trying to remember if she'd ever let it slip. She was almost convinced that she hadn't. But she'd been willing to give him the benefit of the doubt, until she'd seen that man outside the apartment building. Then, every suspicion she'd ever had about Darrin came rushing in along with her fear. Somehow her subconscious mind had made a connection between the two things. She didn't understand why, but she couldn't ignore her instincts.

Shaking his head, he dropped into a chair. "You lost me, Cathy."

"You knew where to have your brother check the records for a suit for Angel's custody. How?"

"What does this have to do with anything?"

He was good at evading questions; she'd noticed that before. "Dammit! Answer me!"

He took a deep breath. "Early in our relationship, you mentioned California."

"When?"

"I think it was the night I first kissed you, though it might have been another time." He smiled ruefully. "I didn't know I'd be expected to account for every scrap of conversation that ever passed between us." He threw his hands out in a helpless gesture. "What brought this on all of a sudden?"

He looked dismayed. Her confidence wavered. What in God's name did she think he was guilty of? she asked herself as she pressed her cold hands to her cheeks. He had a book deadline, yet she'd sensed he hadn't been writing lately. But what did she know about how a writer worked? She'd heard of writer's block; she supposed every writer had to deal with it at one time or another. She knew he'd been working on a book when they met. She'd seen part of his manuscript. He'd signed a six-month apartment lease. It couldn't all be an elaborate ruse. No, that was ridiculous.... Wasn't it?

She forced herself to take deep, even breaths, until she felt calmer. "I'm not sure," she said finally. "It must be that man. He *was* watching the apartment, Darrin. He probably still is."

He stood abruptly and headed for the door.

Alarmed by his suddenly grim expression, she asked, "Where are you going?"

"To reconnoiter the building and the grounds." He slipped the bolt on the door.

"Wait, Darrin! He might have a gun. Take mine."

He hesitated, then picked up the .22, checked the safety and dropped it into his pocket. "I won't be gone long."

Hugging herself, she sank into a corner of the couch. What if Darrin was attacked? She should have called the police. But the police wouldn't take her seriously unless she explained why she was so sure she and Angel were in danger. And then it would all go into a written record that could be seen by the wrong eyes. Frank's organization had eyes everywhere.

She shuddered and cupped her elbows with her hands. Shutting her eyes, she forced her mind to focus on facts. She had seen the same man outside the gallery and later, near the apartment building. He'd carried binoculars. That was the sum and substance of the facts. Her mind had built those facts into a conspiracy involving everyone from Frank to Darrin. Might as well have thrown in Gwen Nettleton and the kitchen sink.

She had lived too long with fear. Was it finally driving her crazy?

Darrin circled A-wing, hugging the darkness. He almost missed the guard, who was sitting behind a crepe myrtle bush, well hidden from view, now that it was too late. He must have found a peep hole for himself through the bush, where he could keep an eye on Cathy's apartment with his binoculars. He didn't hear Darrin slip up behind him.

Not bothering with the .22, Darrin squatted and jabbed a finger against the back of the guard's neck. "Don't move. Just listen."

"What—?" the guard croaked in a shrill falsetto. He sounded young and scared.

"I'm not here to hurt you. You've been made. The lady saw you. Twice, for God's sake."

"Jeez, you scared the crap out of me. This isn't my usual line of work. My uncle was supposed to come, but he's sick. He didn't want to lose the job, so he asked me to stand in for him this once. Jeez, I knew I shoulda said no. Who *are* you?"

"Brown will vouch for me. Tell that to the security firm when you call them, which you are going to do immediately after you get the hell away from here."

"*Who?* I don't understand," the guard quavered.

"You are to leave now," Darrin repeated. "Call the security firm and tell them to replace you with a more experienced guard. Then you stay as far away from the woman and child as you can get. Got all that?"

"I guess so . . . but—"

"Then get out of here," Darrin ordered. He removed his finger from the guard's neck. "Now."

Not inclined to argue any further, the young man scrambled to his feet and ran away from the apartment building. Darrin heard his running feet splatting softly across the dark grounds of the adjacent hotel. At least, he'd had the foresight to wear rubber-soled shoes, Darrin thought. He waited until he could no longer hear a whisper of the guard's retreat before completing his circuit of the apartment building.

When Darrin returned to the apartment fifteen minutes later, Cathy hadn't moved from the sofa. At his knock, she leaped to her feet and ran to the door.

"It's Darrin," he whispered. "Let me in."

She dealt with the chain and locks, and he stepped inside. While she resecured the door, he went to the lamp table and laid the gun on it. When he turned around, she was leaning back against the door, watching him tensely.

"No one's out there," he said shortly. "And I found no sign that anyone had been there."

"I saw him," she said defensively.

"I'm not contradicting you." He went to her, reached for her. She came into his arms after only the slightest hesitation.

She clutched his shirt and pressed against him as if for warmth. "I've decided to take some time off work," she murmured. "I want to be with Angel."

He ran his hands slowly down her back, molding her to him. "I think that's a good idea."

She tilted her head back and looked at him. "You do?"

He heard the surprise in her voice. "Yes. You should stay here, and try to relax for Angel's sake."

Her brows drew together. "I have to conquer it somehow, don't I? I don't want to communicate my negative emotions to Angel."

He took her face in his hands. "You can stay at my place, if you'd feel safer there."

She smiled. "Thank you, but things will seem more routine for Angel in her own home."

"Then I'll be around a lot. I can shop for groceries and run any other errands you want. You can depend on me, Cathy."

She would because she had no other choice. There was no one else she could turn to. She looked up at him, pale, soft, vulnerable.

"I'll sleep on your couch tonight. I may even make you breakfast in the morning."

It was his way of saying that he only wanted to be there for her, without adding to the pressure she was under. He understood her. She dropped her head and snuggled against him. "I'm taking you away from your work."

He tilted her chin and lowered his head. "You're more important to me than work," he murmured against her lips. "All you need to worry about right now is getting some sleep."

"It's too early for sleep." She smiled softly.

He brought his hand up to touch her face. She kissed the fingertips. "Turn out the lights," she murmured.

He circled the room, flipping the switches, then opened the blinds to admit the moonlight. When he finished, she was lying on the couch, waiting for him. "Hold me," she whispered.

She scooted over and he lay beside her. "Don't be afraid, love."

"I'm not afraid when I'm with you." Her tongue traced his lips, and his heartbeat became thunder in his chest.

In the darkness he could see the pale, moonlit oval of her face. His mouth captured hers and instantly he lost himself.

Chapter 13

Later, after Cathy slept, Darrin did bed down on the couch—for a part of the night. But the couch was too soft for comfort and when he awoke at 2:00 a.m., he tossed his pillow and quilt to the floor and spent the remainder of the night there.

When next he awoke, light glowed around the edges of the window blinds. The apartment was silent; Cathy and Angel were still sleeping. He pulled on his shirt and jeans and stowed the quilt and pillow in the hall linen closet. After washing his face and hands at the kitchen sink, he riffled through the refrigerator and pantry to see what was available for breakfast.

He put together pancake batter from a mix and found the griddle. He fried bacon and transferred it to a paper-towel lined plate to drain. When he heard Cathy in the shower, he started her pancakes. As he was arranging her breakfast on a tray, he heard the shower go off.

When he entered the bedroom, she was coming out of the bathroom in her robe. Her skin glowed, still flushed from the shower, and she'd turbaned her wet hair in a white towel. He was relieved to see that she appeared rested.

She smiled as he entered. "Good morning."

"Your breakfast, madame."

"Oh, lovely." She hopped back into bed and smoothed the sheet over her legs. "Have you eaten already?"

He bent to set the tray in her lap and kissed her, lingering over her smiling, uplifted mouth before settling on the edge of the bed and reaching for the second cup of coffee on the tray. "I'll eat later, with Angel."

She buttered the pancakes and poured maple syrup from a small pitcher. "You even warmed the syrup." She gave him a teasing look over the rim of her coffee cup. "Have you done this before?"

"I was a waiter in a former life."

She raised a brow and cut into the pancakes with her fork. "Don't evade the question. I'm talking about this life, as you very well know. Tell me about the other lucky women you've served breakfast in bed."

He took a sip of coffee, then grinned at her. "I don't remember."

She lifted both brows at the same time. "A selective memory. How convenient."

"Yes, isn't it?"

She laughed. "You never answer questions you don't want to answer." She ate a bite of pancake, declared it delicious and cut another bite.

"You're fairly good at that yourself."

Sobering, she gazed at him for an instant, then took another bite. He switched the subject, wanting to bring the smile back to her eyes. "Did you sleep well?"

"Yes, surprisingly. It must have been knowing you were here." Her face became even graver. "But I still have the same feeling I had yesterday, as though things are closing in on me. As though something is going to happen soon, something unpleasant."

He touched her cheek gently. "I'll be here for as long as you want me."

She caught his hand, pressing it hard against her cheek. Her eyes looked misty when she lifted her lashes to meet his gaze. "Thank you."

They sat like that for a moment until the sounds from Angel's bedroom reached them. Darrin set his cup on the tray. "Take your time. I'll head off Angel and feed her."

He closed the bedroom door quietly behind him and almost immediately Cathy heard him talking to Angel in the bedroom down the hall. Angel's laughter made it clear how pleased she was to see him. He was wonderful with her.

Cathy never would have believed, when she first met him, that he had this domestic side. Even Frank hadn't had such an easy relationship with his daughter. When he was at home, he hadn't spent much time with Angel, though occasionally he seemed to realize he'd been remiss and overcompensated by lavishing Angel with gifts. Cathy could feel herself tensing inside, just thinking about Frank. She forced him from her mind by replacing him with Darrin.

She couldn't keep on telling herself that what Darrin didn't know wouldn't hurt him. She couldn't keep him in the dark about Frank much longer. It's not fair to Darrin, she berated herself, as rationalizations, excuses for keeping silent, immediately crowded into her mind. She set the tray aside and went into the bathroom to dry her hair.

Staring into her own eyes reflected in the bathroom mirror, she lifted the blowing hair dryer in one hand and a brush in the other. The sound of the dryer shut out the talk and laughter and left her with only her thoughts.

Darrin had said he'd be there for as long as she wanted him, but the promise had been made without his knowing what it could entail. He had a right to make an informed decision as to whether to risk staying in Cathy's and Angel's lives.

Oh, God, how she dreaded it, though. But she sensed somehow that there wasn't much time left for procrastination. Her stomach contracted sickeningly, but the decision was made. She would tell Darrin everything the next time they were alone without likelihood of interruption.

Darrin left at noon to run errands and take care of some business of his own. He didn't return until after Cathy and Angel had eaten dinner. So there was no opportunity to talk privately until after nine, when Angel went to bed.

By that time, Cathy was so anxious and tense that she couldn't be still. After checking to make sure Angel was asleep, she returned to the living room. She bypassed the couch on which Darrin lounged, leafing idly through a magazine, and went to the corner cabinet. "Would you like a drink?"

He dropped the magazine on the coffee table and watched her nervously finger a cut-glass decanter.

She'd been on edge ever since he returned to the apartment. He'd talked to Vector again and thought he'd finally gotten through to the man; he wasn't going to waltz out of that cell without giving Darrin something valuable in return. Though worried, Vector still wasn't being very helpful. Darrin had left him with instructions to try to come up with anything he might have heard, no matter how insignificant it had seemed at the time, that would give them a clue as to where Kampion was hiding.

"Not now," he said. "You go ahead, though."

She fingered the decanter again, then closed the cabinet door. "No, I don't really want anything."

"Come here."

She shook her head and sat down in an armchair, immediately jumped up again and circled the coffee table and sofa. She stopped halfway between the back of the sofa and the kitchen door, as though she'd forgotten where she'd meant to go.

"It's all right, honey," he said gently. "You and Angel are safe here."

She crossed her arms, gripping her elbows, as though for something to hold on to. She was going to come apart if she didn't tell him.

"No, we aren't—" she took a breath and forced herself to finish "—and neither are you."

Frowning, he started to rise.

"No! Stay over there, please...." It would be easier, she thought, if he weren't touching her.

He stayed. "Cathy..."

She looked at him, her eyes miserable and afraid. Abruptly, she retraced her steps to the cabinet, poured some brandy, lifted the snifter in two hands and drank. "I've decided to tell you about Frank, Angel's father." She took another swallow of brandy and set the snifter on the nearest table.

Darrin had wanted her to tell him for so long, but now he had an impulse to stop her. Her pinched expression worried him. She was too upset, and he didn't think he could stand to let her put herself through this. But he kept silent, knowing that he had to stand it. This moment had been inevitable from the day they met.

"He's, well, I guess he's what you'd call a gangster. No, he *is* a gangster." She watched his face for the beginning of shock and disillusionment, but his expression showed nothing beyond an intense sort of alertness. She swallowed and went on. "I didn't know it when I married him. I'd seen his pictures in the newspaper, in articles about charity functions and at preopening galas for important gallery shows." She began to pace as she talked, dragging a hand through her hair.

"Honey—" He started to go to her, but she whirled and sent him such a frantic look that he changed his mind.

"I can't live with this any longer," she cried, and her voice broke. She clutched the back of a chair and took a moment to compose herself. "Don't you understand? It's poisoning me. I have to get it out."

"I hate seeing you in such pain."

Her face softened for an instant, and then she seemed to gather herself together and went on. "I was twenty-two, but much younger than that in many ways. I took a degree in art history from a small liberal arts college. When I met Frank, I was working in a San Francisco gallery. My title was assistant to the curator, but I was really a general flunky. I did whatever the curator didn't want to do. I loved it.''

She continued to pace as she talked, her fingers combing through her hair or lacing and unlacing themselves at her waist, never still. "Frank had donated a large sum of money for remodeling a wing of the museum. The directors threw a lavish reception, with Frank as guest of honor, when the wing was reopened. I met him that night.''

Now that the words were finally coming, there was no stopping them. They poured out of her, mercilessly honest. She didn't hold back, didn't try to explain or excuse herself. She told him how awed she'd been by the sophisticated older man, the wealthy patron of the arts, how flattered she'd been by his attention, which had started the next day with two dozen roses delivered to her at the museum. Frank Kampion had wooed her with an old-world courtliness foreign to her experience, to her generation.

She'd been skeptical at first. Of course she had. What could such a man see in a penniless orphan such as she? He told her he loved her many times before she would let herself believe it. He let her set the pace of their relationship, taking his cues from her. She never felt any pressure from him. He didn't take her to see the mansion where he lived until they'd known each other for six months. They didn't sleep together until they'd known each other for eight months, not until after he'd proposed to her and she'd accepted. She didn't meet his mother until two weeks before the wedding. Frank took care of all the arrangements for the ceremony, reception and honeymoon in Spain and Morocco.

Angel was born two years later, and Cathy had been so happy that it frightened her sometimes. What had she done to deserve such happiness? Three years had passed in this way, the only serious shadow on her rose-colored life being Frank's frequent trips away from home—to take care of his various business enterprises all over the world, he told her. She had no reason to doubt what he said.

Looking back, she knew that almost from the beginning of the marriage, there had been clues pointing to the fact that her husband was not what he seemed. Small things. But she had not seen them. Perhaps she hadn't wanted to.

What finally began to penetrate the dreamworld in which she lived were the "business associates" who came to the house to meet with Frank. They never stayed for a meal, nor were they invited to the grand parties Frank gave in San Francisco's finest hotels twice a year or the small, intimate dinners at the mansion for a few friends, which Cathy preferred. It was a mistake to mix business with pleasure, Frank often said.

There were always several men around. House servants, groundsmen, and the guards Frank insisted were necessary because of his valuable collection of artwork. Cathy got used to them. So, for a long time, she paid little attention to the other, dark-suited men who came and went at odd hours. When she did begin to really look at them, usually from a bedroom or nursery window, they struck her as somehow furtive. Their eyes darted everywhere as they got out of their cars, before they proceeded to Frank's office suite through an outside door at the back of the house.

Cathy never saw any of them without his suit jacket until one very hot summer afternoon when a man called Burke returned to his car after a meeting with Frank. Before getting in the car, he loosened his tie and removed his jacket, laying it carefully in the back seat. He closed the back door and turned to open the driver's door. As he did so, Cathy was stunned to see a gun in a shoulder holster strapped over his businessman's white shirt.

She didn't mention the gun to Frank. She'd never kept anything from her husband before, and she didn't understand why she did then, except that some instinct for caution kept her silent.

After that, she noticed other things. Suspicion and distrust, once having taken root, grew until one day she lifted a receiver in the bedroom she shared with her husband and overheard a conversation between Frank and another man concerning the delivery and distribution of a large shipment of cocaine. The phone in Frank's office was supposed to be a private line, but men from the telephone company had been there that day, installing several new phones and, through a misunderstanding or a mistake, the phones in the master bedroom suite and those in Frank's offices had been connected to the same line.

So absorbed was she in the telling, Cathy seemed almost to have forgotten Darrin was there. Her words trailed off as she turned around to pace back across the room. Silent tears trickled down her cheeks. She seemed unaware of them.

Darrin reached her in three strides. "Enough, Cathy. It's enough." He folded her trembling body in his arms.

She pushed against him and stared up at him, blinking away the haze that covered her eyes. "Let me finish," she pleaded shakily.

Poison, she had said, and she had to get it out. More tears spilled. He swallowed and pulled her gently back to him. "Let me hold you, then."

She sagged against him, all the fight going out of her. A shudder shook her and she was quiet for a while, her head resting on his shoulder. He stroked her hair with great tenderness. What could he say to make this easier for her?

Finally, she took a deep breath and told him about the last year of her marriage—her announcement that she was leaving and taking Angel, his attempts to talk her out of it and finally the warning that if she left him she would leave her daughter, as well, that she would never see Angel again. The long pretense, the escape, the flight to Houston, the "misplacement" of the court's notice of divorce hearing with the help of a maid, and the second flight to St. Thomas.

When she stopped, he continued to hold her and stroke her hair. His throat ached, and he didn't trust himself to speak. The silence lengthened.

"For a long time," she said at last, "I couldn't bring myself to tell you. I thought I was protecting you, but really I was terrified of what you'd think, that you'd feel differently about me afterward." Her voice quavered on the last word. "Do you?"

Darrin's arms around her tightened. At last he knew what to say. "I loved you before, and I love you now. Nothing can change that."

She lifted her face. She was crying again, but this time she was smiling through the tears. "Oh Darrin... I love you, too. So very much. Oh..." A trembling sigh escaped her. She planted a wet kiss on his jaw and chin. "I've wanted to hear you say you loved me for so long."

"I wanted to, but it never seemed to be the right time."

"It feels so good not to have any secrets between us."

He didn't respond. Instead, he caught her face in his hands to stop the roaming of her mouth. She didn't seem to notice the omission, was too lost in the savage possession of his mouth to notice anything else.

The kiss was salty with her tears.

Three days passed. Cathy seemed a little less tense each day, but she didn't mention returning to work. Darrin was with her as much as he could be. He talked to the prisoner again at the police station. Confinement was getting to Vector, and he tried to reconstruct verbatim the few conversations he'd had with an employee or acquaintance of Kampion. He recalled mention being made of a mountain retreat—in Colorado, he thought. But that site had been under surveillance by the bureau for months. Kampion wasn't there.

Another time, Vector said, one of Kampion's bodyguards had told him Kampion was leaving the next day, going to some kind of meeting. He wasn't taking his wife and child, the bodyguard had said, from which Vector had deduced that Kampion was going to conduct drug business.

"He didn't say where this meeting was going to take place?" Darrin asked. He was only going through the motions by that time. He didn't think Vector knew anything that would be helpful in finding Kampion. Darrin was convinced that if he did, he'd have spilled by now. Apparently Vector was mildly claustrophobic. He looked haggard. The cell was definitely getting on his nerves.

Vector shook his head helplessly.

"Did he say whether Kampion was driving or flying?"

Another shake of the head.

"Well," Darrin sighed, "I'll come back tomorrow."

"Wait!" Vector said desperately. "Give me a few more minutes. I think he did mention a place...a town maybe." He squeezed his eyes shut in an effort to concentrate.

"Since you don't remember the name," Darrin suggested, "could it have been one you haven't heard before?"

Vector nodded slowly. "Yeah . . . I think that was it. It sounded . . . wait a minute. It reminded me of the Bible."

"The Bible," Darrin said blankly.

"Yeah," Vector said eagerly. "My mother used to take me to Sunday school when I was a little kid. It reminded me of something I heard there."

Darrin stared at him, trying to picture Vector as a child, dressed in short pants and a white shirt, clutching a tiny New Testament in his pudgy little hand. Impossible.

"Didn't you ever go to Sunday school?" Vector asked.

"With my grandparents."

"Well, can't you remember the names of some of those towns in the Bible?"

"Uh, Jerusalem. Bethlehem. Sodom and Gomorrah." This was hopeless.

Vector hung on each word, then said unhappily, "I don't think it was one of those. Name some more."

"Kampion has never been to that part of the world," Darrin said in exasperation. "I'm wasting my time here."

"I didn't say it *was* one of those places. Just that it reminded me of one of them. Go ahead and name some more."

Hell, this was getting him nowhere, Darrin thought. He stared at a wall and tried to resurrect those long ago Sunday mornings in a little Iowa town. Mrs. Burgess had been the teacher. She had always smelled like flowers. "Athens," he said finally. "Corinth."

"Wasn't there a town where a bunch of people marched around the walls and they fell down?"

"Jericho," Darrin said promptly. He remembered Mrs. Burgess telling that story. The people had blown trumpets. She'd brought a real trumpet to class and even blown a few notes on it, to illustrate.

"Jericho," Vector said musingly. "That might have been it. Yeah, I think it was Jericho."

Darrin suspected the man was so desperate he was making the whole thing up. He'd never heard of any Jericho except the one in the Bible. He thought it was part of Jordan now.

"Does that help you?" Vector asked hopefully.

"I don't know. I'll make some inquiries. You'll be hearing from me." He left the interrogation room, sure there was nothing useful buried in Vector's memory. He'd tell Brown to have the police hold Vector a couple more days. When they let him go, he'd be put under close surveillance.

Back at his apartment, he phoned Rainey, whom he'd been keeping informed of his meetings with Vector. Jericho didn't ring any bells with Rainey, either, but he said he'd assign somebody to look up every damn town on the globe with any name like it. What else did they have?

Relieved of that probably useless bit of information, Darrin decided to invite Cathy and Angel over for dinner. They needed to get out of their apartment, even if it was only to leave A-wing for B-wing.

Chapter 14

If Darrin hadn't been emotionally involved in the Kampion case, he would not have been so careless. It had never happened before. It should not have happened this time, he berated himself over and over. When it was too late.

Cathy and Angel were glad to get out of the apartment. "I never realized before how small it is," Cathy said. Angel was beginning to get cranky. She missed Dawn and Eric and didn't understand why Cathy now refused to let her play outside with them.

Cathy tossed a salad in Darrin's kitchen, while he cooked steaks on the patio grill. Angel ran from the house to the patio and back again repeatedly, elated with even that small amount of freedom. "Slow down," Cathy kept saying, for all the good it did.

"Darrin wants a root beer," Angel announced on her next trip to the kitchen. "He said I can have one, too." She ran to the refrigerator and took out two of the canned drinks. Cathy popped the tabs for her. Angel tipped one of the cans up and promptly poured half of it down the front of her dress.

"It's cold!" she shrieked.

Cathy grabbed a towel and mopped up the puddle at Angel's feet. She had to bite her tongue to hold back a harsh reprimand, reminding herself that Angel was only three, and it wasn't her fault that her pent-up energy had to finally come out.

"Darrin," Cathy called, "I'm going to have to take Angel home and get her some dry clothes."

Darrin appeared at the open patio door. "What's going on, big'n?"

"I had an accident," Angel wailed, close to tears. "My dress got all wet." The smallest things had brought her to tears today.

"Put one of my T-shirts on her," Darrin suggested.

Angel giggled. "Can I, Mommy?" She loved dressing up in adult clothes. Gwen kept a drawer full of old dresses and jewelry for Angel and Dawn to entertain themselves with.

Darrin grinned at Cathy. "They're in the top left dresser drawer, Mommy."

"Oh, why not," Cathy said, laughing. Darrin disappeared, going to tend to the steaks.

Cathy picked through the stack of white T-shirts and chose the oldest looking one. When she turned around, Angel was looking at her with big eyes. She'd taken Darrin's attaché case from the closet. It had fallen open, or Angel had opened it, and papers were strewn across the carpet.

"I didn't mean to, Mommy," Angel said in a small voice.

Cathy sighed. "You know you shouldn't get into other people's things, sweetheart. Set it down and I'll put the papers back. Here, let's get that wet dress off."

Subdued, Angel set the case down. After stripping off the wet dress, Cathy dropped the T-shirt over Angel's head. It barely hung on her shoulders and the tail dragged along the carpet. Angel thought it was wonderful. "Go and hang your dress on a rack in the bathroom," Cathy said, "and I'll clean up Darrin's papers."

"You won't tell him I spilled them, will you?" Angel asked anxiously.

Cathy hugged her. "No, there's no harm done."

Smiling again, Angel left the room, dragging her wet dress behind her. Cathy bent and began to retrieve the papers, which were sheets of plain white computer paper that had been separated along the perforations. Darrin's manuscript. Over three hundred pages, she realized as she put them back in numerical order. She recognized some of the chapter headings as those she'd seen the first time she'd come to Darrin's apartment, but they'd been on green-and-white lined fanfold paper then. Apparently this was the final copy, and it appeared to be a nearly complete manuscript.

Odd, she mused, as she picked up the last of the pages. When she found that last number sheet, she saw that the manuscript was indeed finished. "The End" was typed in bold print halfway down the page.

How could Darrin have accomplished so much during the past several weeks? He'd said he was blocked. Thoughtfully, she righted the attaché case and started to place the manuscript inside. That was when she saw the second manuscript. It appeared to be another computer book. Different from the first one, she realized as she leafed through the pages. It had a different title and chapter headings. The name beneath the title on the first page of each manuscript was Kent Boyle.

She frowned in perplexity. Kent was probably Darrin's middle name, she told herself, the name he used on his books. But he couldn't possibly have written two books in the time she'd known him, even if he'd worked at it twelve hours a day. Yet here were two completed manuscripts.

It made no sense to her. Well, she wasn't going to figure it out by staring at the manuscripts. She'd ask Darrin about it. She was sure there must be a simple explanation. Maybe the second manuscript was a book Darrin had written previously, not the second book of his current contract. That has to be it, she told herself as she lifted both manuscripts to drop them back into the case.

Oh, no. The bottom of the case had come loose. One corner was sticking up. Angel must have damaged it. She set the manuscripts down on the carpet and tried to push the loose corner back in place. But there seemed to be an obstruction; she couldn't push the corner back down. It looked as though she'd have to pull the panel all the way out to get it back in properly.

She worked two fingers beneath the loose corner and tugged gently. The panel lifted easily at the top, though it seemed firmly attached at the bottom. Apparently it hadn't been glued in properly.

She pulled the panel up far enough to peek beneath it to see if something had fallen behind it and was preventing the panel from fitting properly.

She sucked in a breath. For an instant, she thought she must be seeing an optical illusion. But it wasn't. It was a gun, concealed in a secret compartment beneath a false bottom in Darrin's attaché case.

She couldn't believe it! After he'd lectured her on the hazards of owning a gun. Had he had it all along? But how had he gotten it through customs? No, he must have bought it only recently. Why? Did Darrin know something he wasn't telling her? Had he seen a suspicious character hanging around the apartment building and decided to "protect her" by not telling her?

She stared at the gun a long moment before she realized that it wasn't lying on the bottom of the secret compartment, but on a large manila envelope. Something was very wrong. She knew that, even as she reached for the envelope and opened its clasp. She felt numb, as though she were watching somebody else do it.

Inside were five enlarged color photographs. Her chest constricted painfully as she looked through them, and something hard rose in her throat, as though her contracting chest muscles were squeezing her heart from her body. She felt as though she couldn't get enough air. There was not enough air in the room. In the world.

The photographs were of her, taken before she dyed her hair. Before she left San Francisco.

Her hands shook so violently that she couldn't get the photographs back in the envelope. She gave up trying and left them there in the open attaché case.

"No," she whispered, shocked to hear her own voice. *Oh, God, no...don't let this be happening. Not Darrin...please, not Darrin.*

Her rational mind was no longer functioning. Instinct activated her. Angel was leaving the bathroom as she entered the hall. Cathy wasn't even sure she could speak until she heard herself say, "We have to go home." She grabbed Angel up into her arms and ran into the living room.

"Mommy, why are you crying?"

She hadn't known she was. "We can't talk now," Cathy managed jerkily. "We have to—" But words failed her, as she reached the door and opened it.

"I don't want to go home yet," Angel wailed.

Cathy pushed her daughter's head down on her shoulder and ran.

When Darrin came inside with the grilled steaks on a platter Cathy and Angel weren't in the kitchen. He set the steaks down and went into the living room. "Hey, where is everybody?"

They weren't there, either, and nobody answered him. Frowning, he started down the hall toward his bedroom. He was halfway there when the telephone rang. He entered the bedroom, going around the bed to the extension on the bedside table. Where the hell were Cathy and Angel?

He snatched up the receiver. "Yes."

"Boyle, that you?"

It was Rainey. "Who else?"

"Yeah." Rainey coughed, then said, "Jerico, Colombia."

It was an instant before Darrin knew what he was talking about. His mind was still on Cathy and Angel. Something was wrong. He could feel it.

"One of those arrogant drug lords who're trying to run the country has a compound outside of town. Kampion could be there. I'm taking a team down. If you can make connections to the Miami airport by tomorrow at 6:00 p.m., you can hook up with us."

"I'll try," Darrin said distractedly. He would worry about it later. Right now he had something else on his mind. "Look for me when you see me," he said abruptly and hung up.

It wasn't until he came around from behind the bed that he saw the attaché case lying open on the floor near the closet. The photographs of Cathy were fanned out inside it, and the scene formed crystal clear in his mind. Cathy opening the briefcase, finding the secret compartment, seeing the gun and the manila envelope. Taking the pictures out . . .

Oh, God, where was she? What was she thinking?

He raced from the apartment all the way to A-wing and Cathy's door.

Cathy was throwing things into suitcases, paying no attention to how, just so long as she could get packed and get out. The .22 automatic lay on the bedside table. She'd dispose of it at the airport before she went through the checkpoint.

She'd gone directly to Gwen's from Darrin's apartment and left Angel, with no explanation except that she'd be back for her within the hour.

She had to stop frequently to wipe her eyes with a hand towel from the bathroom. Get it over with, she told herself, and then, don't let me cry in front of Angel.

She was in pain, more excruciating than any she'd ever known. Pain so severe that it blocked out fear and all other emotions. She was cold. Would she ever be warm again?

The pounding on the apartment door made her jerk violently. She reached for the gun and crept into the living room.

"Cathy! Let me in. Please let me talk to you, let me explain." Darrin's voice was the voice of a stranger.

She froze, facing the door. With the .22 clutched in two shaking hands, she waited.

"Cathy! I know you're in there! Answer me, dammit!"

Her eyes were dry now. She was finished with crying. She would do what she had to do, and she would shed no more tears. With a shuddering sigh, she cried, "I'm holding the .22, Darrin. Don't try to force your way in."

"My God!" His voice was anguished. "Listen to me, sweetheart. It isn't what you think. I'm a government agent. I couldn't tell you. . . . I'm sorry, Cathy."

Sorry, she thought as she slowly lowered the gun. A government agent? Maybe later, she would be able to understand. Understand but not forgive. She had to convince him she'd talk to him later, if only he'd leave now so that she and Angel could get away.

"Cathy, did you hear me?"

"I heard you," she said unsteadily.

"Let me in."

"No! I can't talk to you now. Give me time to think."

After a moment, he said reluctantly, "An hour, Cathy. Then I'll be back and I'm coming in, one way or the other."

Numb, she listened to his footsteps recede. She had little emotion left to spend. Hurriedly, she returned to the bedroom, finished packing and closed the suitcases. Ten minutes later, she was ringing Gwen's doorbell. Twenty minutes later, she and Angel were in a taxi on the way to the airport.

Chapter 15

One year later

Cathy gazed at the gray mist through the bookshop's steamy window. The blurred image of a tall man approached the pub across the way, walking briskly. He wore a gray overcoat with upturned collar. He pulled open the pub door and merged with the murky rectangular opening as he entered, the door swinging shut behind him.

Something about the way he'd moved held her there for another moment after he'd disappeared. Turning away, she suddenly knew why his walk had caught her attention. It reminded her of Darrin's.

Squaring her shoulders in the soft blue sweater, she went to the tiny alcove separating the bookshop proper from Mr. Brenner's office, and switched on the electric hotplate to heat water for tea.

The elderly owner of the shop had turned her into a tea lover. At first, it had simply seemed easier to drink the tea Mr. Brenner brewed twice a day, rather than bother with coffee and another pot.

She'd developed a taste for it and now rarely drank more than a single cup of coffee with breakfast. She'd changed in other ways, too. She was known as Cathy Kampion now and her hair had returned to its natural platinum blond. She no longer lived with fear. Her life had taken on a serenity that she prized, having learned what it was like to live without it.

The first three months they'd lived here had been the hardest, she mused, as she took down the canister of specially blended teas, filled the perforated metal ball and dropped it into the china pot. She smiled, remembering Mr. Brenner's oft repeated statement that tea bags were an abomination to a tea connoisseur.

Yes, the first three months had been grim. There had been a few times in those early days when she'd wondered if her depression would ever lift. Angel had helped. So had the city.

She'd wanted a place that wouldn't bring back any memories, and London was as different from Charlotte Amalie as could be found in the English-speaking world. Slowly, her depression had lifted, and she'd learned to laugh again.

Now another autumn was upon her, almost before she knew it. She'd grown accustomed to the fog and damp and thought how lovely and green England was in the spring. She felt comfortable there now, and Angel had picked up the accent quickly. Her daughter sounded like a native these days. In September, she'd started at a private school near their flat, and she loved it and the new friends she'd made there.

Since Mr. Brenner was away today visiting his son, Cathy readied only one cup, filling it when the tea had steeped the proper length of time. She carried her tea back to the front of the shop. There had been a midday rush and a few customers always came in later after their day's work. Until then, she thought she'd have time to rearrange the history section.

As she began taking books off the shelves, the image of the man in the overcoat flickered through her mind. Sighing, she told herself that the odd thought of Darrin was bound to come into her mind occasionally. One did not forget the past, even when one had closed a door on it.

Nor did she want to forget everything about her former life. Soon after arriving in London, she'd subscribed to the *New York Times* to keep up with news from home. It was in the *Times* that she'd read of Frank's extradition from Colombia, his arrest, trial and imprisonment. One edition had even carried a grainy picture of Frank entering a federal courthouse with his attorney. She'd disposed of that edition quickly, lest Angel saw it.

She would tell Angel about her father one day, of course, when she was old enough to understand and accept it. Angel never spoke of Frank, though, once in a while, especially in the beginning, she asked about Darrin. Cathy's vague replies hadn't really satisfied Angel, and lately she'd given up asking. Now her mind was chock-full of school and her new friends.

Cathy wanted Angel to know her own country, too, and she was sure they'd go back. One day.

As she lifted the last few books from the top shelf of the history section, the bell on the shop door tinkled. It was Mrs. Mills, a retired schoolmarm who lived in the neighborhood. Mrs. Mills was widowed and childless. She was lonely, Cathy thought.

"You're just in time to have a cup of tea with me," Cathy called.

"Grand, luvee. We'll have a bite of my biscuits, too." She waved the cookie tin as Cathy came to help her off with her coat.

Darrin nursed two glasses of beer for half the afternoon, while keeping his eyes on the bookshop across the street from the pub. Since there wasn't much traffic on this dreary day, the proprietor seemed content to leave him be.

It had taken him months to find Cathy and Angel, after Kampion's trial and sentencing. Because Cathy hadn't booked the flight out of St. Thomas in the name of either Prentiss or Kampion, it had been impossible to trace her from there.

Even when one of the many feelers he'd put out through contacts in bureau offices around the world finally paid off, he didn't try to make contact right away. Instead, he began laying out a methodical plan to wind up his unfinished business at the bureau. His final assignment had been to identify the person in the Washington office who had leaked the information that the agent handling the Kampion investigation was in St. Thomas. It had turned out to be a computer programmer whose lover was a small-time hood with mob connections.

Darrin had resigned a month ago. Having accumulated enough savings to live on for a while, he'd sold his car and given up his Georgetown apartment. He planned to enter the private practice of law at some point in the future, but he couldn't concentrate on that until he'd seen Cathy.

He didn't want to talk to her in the bookshop where they'd be interrupted, so he waited until he saw her come out of the shop in a hooded raincoat and turn to lock the door behind her. As she set off down the street, he threw some pound notes on the table and left.

He crossed the street, weaving between lanes of traffic. Cathy hadn't looked up. She walked head down, protecting her face from the wet drizzle.

"Cathy," he said as he fell into step beside her.

She glanced toward him and froze.

Darrin watched the color leave her face, except for feverishly bright spots high on her cheeks. He saw shock in her eyes, and panic. The panic made his throat thicken painfully. She stopped in the middle of the walk, and her hands clutched her purse against her breast. The heavy flow of pedestrians on their way home from work continued to pass by on either side of them.

Help me, God, she thought frantically. Tell me what to do, what to say.

He watched her scrambling thoughts reflected in her pinched face, his gaze riveted on the dark blue eyes. The wisps of hair escaping the hood of her raincoat were the striking platinum that he knew was natural. *How could he have forgotten how beautiful she was?* She had been lovely even with the dyed brown hair and the cloud of fear always waiting to flood her eyes. But she was so beautiful now that he couldn't stop staring. It seemed he had waited an eternity to see her again, always imagining time would have healed the hurt he'd caused her, that her face would be lighted from within by joy when she caught sight of him. But there was no joy in her now, only confusion and dismay. Because of what he had done. Despair overwhelmed him. He didn't know how he could go on if the months of searching and the total rearrangement of his life had been for nothing.

The color in her cheeks was fading. Her skin was as flawlessly perfect as he remembered. Was it as soft? Would she turn away in revulsion if he touched her? He didn't dare risk it and could only stare at her.

Cathy hugged her purse to her body so tightly that her arms ached. Everywhere else, she felt numb. One of them had to say something. She prayed her voice would sound steady and sure.

"Hello, Darrin." She forced her arms not to grip so tightly, but her nails bit into the leather of her purse. "What are you doing in London? Pretending to be a writer again?"

He kept his hands jammed deep into the pockets of his overcoat. If he let them leave his pockets, he was afraid he wouldn't be able to stop himself touching her. "I came to see you. I've searched the world over for you."

His voice sounded harsh with the anguish of being separated from her for a full year, the months and months when he feared he'd never see her again. Followed by the months of planning and preparation so that he could go to her free of any other claim or responsibility. He had meant to be quiet and reasonable, but he could not stand face-to-face with her and remain calm.

"I came all this way to get away from you, Darrin." Cathy managed to keep her eyes level. "I'm sorry you've tracked me down. You've spent a lot of time and money for nothing."

"No! It can't be for nothing." His voice had risen to such a pitch that people all around them looked their

way curiously. How could he lose his temper with her, after aching for so long to see her? But he couldn't help it. He was desperate. His life had turned to dead ashes without her.

Was there nothing left of the feelings she'd had for him? After what they'd had together, how could she speak to him in that toneless voice, as though he were a tiresome stranger who was delaying her?

"The last year has been sheer hell for me."

"It's been a real barrel of laughs for me," she flared, her eyes fired with sudden fury.

At least, she's feeling *something*, he thought. "Damn it, Cathy...." His hand would not stay in his pocket any longer. It gripped her arm, his voice trailing off as she winced. "Oh, God, I never wanted to hurt you," he said desperately.

"Then I'd hate to be around when you did want to, Darrin." His hold loosened and she pulled her arm free of his fingers. "I have a train to catch."

He moved instantly, blocking her way. "I came to London to talk to you, Cathy, and I'm not leaving until I do."

She stepped back. He kept pace, his jaw set, his expression grim. "Angel's sitter expects me to pick her up in half an hour."

"I'll go with you."

"No!"

He saw the fear leap into her eyes. She didn't want Angel to see him. She didn't want to take him where they lived. How could she be afraid of him? But she was, afraid of how much he could hurt her if she let him back into her life. A long moment passed before he could trust himself to speak.

"Please, Cathy," he said quietly. "Go somewhere with me so we can talk. In God's name, don't send me away without that much, at least."

"You let me love you," she said in a tone of desperate calm, "and you were using me—all the time, you were using me."

"Listen to how it was for me." He was ready to beg if necessary. Whatever pride he'd possessed had been destroyed in the past year. He lifted his hand to touch her again, but let it drop when she stiffened. He had rehearsed for months what he would say when he finally found her, but now there was only one thing he wanted her to hear. "I loved you. I love you now. Listen to me and then if you still feel the same way, I won't bother you again."

"I don't even know what love means to you." Her eyes suddenly filled with angry tears. She wiped them away with the back of her hand. "I have spent a year trying to forget you. I've made a good life for me and Angel. Now you come and just . . . just smash everything I've accomplished."

"No, Cathy. Please, don't say that. . . ." He reached for her but she pushed him away.

"I don't want you to touch me." She wiped away more tears. "All right. There's a restaurant near here. I'll call the sitter and say I'll be late. I'll hear you out, but it isn't going to change one terrible second of the past year."

He followed her to the restaurant, hurrying to keep up with her. She went straight to the telephone and he found a table for them. When she joined him a few minutes later, she'd removed her raincoat. Her beauty almost took his breath. Her hair was a cloud of pale gold framing her face and falling over her shoulders.

The soft blue sweater emphasized the deep blue of her eyes. She sat down across from him, her hands clasped primly in her lap.

"I ordered a bottle of wine. We could wait a bit before ordering dinner, or do it now. It's up to you."

"I don't think I'll be having dinner. I can't stay that long."

The waiter brought the chardonnay. Darrin took the bottle, waving the waiter away, and poured for both of them. All his carefully rehearsed speeches had deserted him. He didn't know where to start, what to say. He had only this one chance.... "When I returned to your apartment that day in Charlotte Amalie and found you'd gone, cleared out..." He faltered. His memory of that moment was as clear as if it had happened yesterday. How could he tell her about the staggering pain that had come when he'd realized she wasn't there, wasn't returning? She had run away again...not from her ex-husband, but from him. Right now she was looking at him as though she wished she hadn't agreed to listen to him. As though she'd rather be anywhere but there with him.

"When I realized you'd gone," he continued, "I almost went crazy. I'd driven away the one person in the world who meant everything to me. I never meant to hurt you, Cathy. You must believe that."

"Why did you lie about who you were? You made love to me...and you kept right on lying, even after you knew I'd fallen in love with you."

"Dear God, I..." He had relived it again and again in the past year, and even now he did not know how he could have done it differently. "I didn't know you were hiding from Kampion when I came to St. Thomas. I didn't know about the divorce. I thought you were hiding from the government agents—from me. I thought Kampion would come to you eventually, or you'd go to him, and when that happened, we'd arrest him." He looked down at his hands, clasped together on the polished tabletop. His knuckles whitened as his grip tightened. "I was the agent on the case. I was doing my job."

"Was sleeping with me part of the job description?"

He stared at his hands. "I never wanted a woman as much as I wanted you. I thought you were waiting for Kampion, and I despised myself, but I still wanted you. I made love to you, believing you were married, knowing it was unconscionable." He looked at her then, his eyes stark with the pain of self-loathing. "I fell in love with you and nothing else mattered. I'm not sure I can ever forgive myself for what I did to you, but I'm asking—begging—you to try to understand."

Cathy had not believed he could reach her ever again. Yet, deep inside her there was a quiver of response to his anguish. She was intimately acquainted with anguish.

She sat in silence for a moment. He had perpetrated an elaborate masquerade for her benefit, had gained her trust and then used that trust to further his investigation. That could never be glossed over.

He had also spent a year searching for her and had come halfway around the world to tell her he loved her and to beg her forgiveness.

She had spent the past year trying to rid herself of the love she'd had for him. She thought she had succeeded. Now, sitting face-to-face with him, seeing him more clearly than she ever had before, she knew she loved him still. Perhaps she always would. Did that mean she was weak? Maybe it only meant that her love was even deeper than she'd imagined.

She wasn't a robot. She was a mere woman, imperfect, flawed. As he was only human, a mere man.

Had her behavior during those weeks in Charlotte Amalie been so exemplary that she could sit in judgment on him?

"Darrin." She waited until his gaze met hers. "Maybe I should have stayed and had it out with you, but when I found the gun and photographs, I panicked."

"You thought I was working for Frank, I know. What else could you think?"

She shook her head. "I wasn't thinking at all. I was in shock."

He stretched out his hand and his fingertips touched hers tentatively. "When you told me you'd divorced him and that he'd send someone after Angel, I should have told you everything right then. Only, I knew what it would do to you to learn who I really was and what I was doing in St. Thomas." His voice roughened with emotion, but he never took his eyes off her face. "I knew I'd lose you, and I couldn't face that. So I let things ride. I must have been deranged. I even told myself that maybe I could leave the bureau and ask you to marry me, and you'd never have to know." He saw her eyes widen in surprise.

"But you found the photographs and I had to tell you who I was. I really believed you when you said we'd talk it out after you'd had time to think. When I came back, you were gone. I went wild. Stormed into Gwen Nettleton's apartment, demanding to know where you'd gone. I made an ass of myself at the airport. All I wanted to do was get my hands on you and force you to listen to me."

She had closed her eyes and now pressed two fingers to the space between her brows. He studied her face. "After I calmed down and regained some sanity, I knew I might have forced you to listen if I'd found you, but I couldn't make things be the way they were before you learned who I was. You trusted me enough to tell me the truth. I was afraid to trust you that much."

She opened her eyes and stared at him. "Until you had to, because the truth finally wasn't as terrible as what I might be thinking. But then it was too late, Darrin. I really don't know what else there is to say."

"You promised to hear me out." She pulled her fingertips away, breaking the fragile contact with his, and he felt the withdrawal like an icy draft. "When I realized I couldn't trace you through the airlines, I threw my things together and went to meet my boss in Miami. From there we flew to Bogotá and met with a high government official to arrange for Frank's extradition. I tried to keep so busy I didn't have time to think of you while the trial was in progress. I wanted to believe I'd succeed in forgetting you altogether in time. Then I'd wake up at night and I'd see your eyes, burning as they did when we made love. I'd heard you saying that no one had ever made you feel that way before."

"Darrin, please don't—"

"I couldn't forget you." He shook his head and leaned toward her, elbows on the table. "Not in a thousand years. I had to find you. And when I did, I cleared everything else out of my life so that I could come to you with nothing pulling me back there. I re-signed from the bureau.''

"Resigned?'' she repeated.

"They tried to make me change my mind. They offered me a sabbatical. Six months, a year. Whatever I needed. But I knew I could never win you back with my job—and the pain that doing it caused you—between us.''

Cathy stared at her untouched wineglass. "You shouldn't have left your job. I won't be made to feel responsible because you decided on a whim to throw away a secure income.''

"I'm in no danger of starving.'' He took one of her hands in his. She let him hold it for a moment before she drew away. "I'm a lawyer, a member of the bar in several states. I'm quite capable of supporting myself—and a family.''

Her eyes darted to his face. "Don't . . .''

"All I'm asking for is another chance. Let me stay here and spend some time with you and Angel. I won't try to pressure you for more than that until you're ready.''

She pressed her hands to her temples. "I may never be ready for more than that.''

He felt a faint quiver of hope. She hadn't said that he couldn't stay, that he couldn't see her. "Then I'll have to learn to live with that.''

She gave him a sharp look. "I don't think you'd be satisfied with that sort of arrangement very long.''

"No,'' he said frankly, "but I can live with it if I have to. I'll be able to see you.''

"I don't know,'' she said hesitantly. "I never thought I'd see you again. After so much time, I thought you'd forgotten me.''

"But I didn't forget. I'm here, and I love you."

"Oh, Darrin...." She leaned her forehead against her hand, covering her eyes. "I'd found some peace. I have friends. I have my daughter and my job and my flat. That's all I want."

"Is it?" he asked quietly.

She lifted her head and her eyes swam with emotion. "Damn you, Darrin. For showing up here and messing up my life again."

"Love isn't neat, Cathy."

She merely looked at him, shaking her head, unable to speak. As the silence between them lengthened, pain crept in and swept through him. He had said everything he knew to say, but he hadn't swayed her. If he left this restaurant without her, he'd never see her again. He'd risked everything to come to her, and he'd lost.

His vision blurred and he looked away from her, blinking to clear it. He saw the two glasses full of white liquid and was surprised to realize that they hadn't touched the wine. "I'll be in town for two or three days." He named the hotel where he was staying. "If I don't hear from you..." He couldn't finish, couldn't bear to hear his voice utter the finality of the words. He rose and turned toward the door.

If you let him go, her heart shouted at her, *you let your love go with him.*

But he used her, betrayed her love.

And he's desperately sorry. He humbled himself to come here and tell you so.

He had almost reached the door when she leaped from her chair and ran after him. "Darrin, wait." When he turned, she was right behind him. "Come home with me. Angel has missed you." She smiled tremulously. "We have both missed you."

"Cathy, you can take longer to think about it. . . ."

"Thinking is what got me where I am now. Maybe I've done too much thinking."

With a moan of relief, he reached for her. "I love you." He kissed her, until they were jostled by a fat, disgruntled man who mumbled that people ought to go home if they had to indulge in such unrestrained behavior.

Cathy turned a smile on the cantankerous gentleman. "Forgive us for blocking your way. We forgot ourselves."

The man humpphed and stomped out. "We'd better leave before we get arrested," Darrin said. He went back after her raincoat, which she'd left on the back of her chair. After helping her into it, he wrapped an arm around her and drew her out of the lighted restaurant into the dark and the mist.

Beneath the restaurant's overhanging eaves, he gave her a feverish kiss as though he could sate a year-long hunger standing there on the public street. At last, he drew back, his eyes dark and intense. "Marry me. We'll live wherever you want. I don't care, as long as you and Angel are there."

"There's so much we need to talk about," she said, "before we talk about marriage."

He swallowed a protest and said instead, "All right. You're calling the shots."

"Give me time to get used to all of this. I don't want to make any more mistakes."

He wanted to say that a future that did not include the two of them together would be the most tragic mistake of all. But he had promised not to press her.

"Nor do I. I made enough in St. Thomas to last a lifetime. I'll try not to mention marriage again for a least twenty-four hours."

She smiled with a despairing shake of her head. "Thank you ever so much."

"In the meantime, I'll concentrate on getting Angel on my side."

"That's dirty pool."

"I know." His boyish grin made her laugh. "Desperate men resort to desperate measures." His grin faded. "I can't live the rest of my life without you. I'll give you all the time you need, but in the end, you'll marry me."

She sighed. "I expect I will," she murmured, and went back into his arms.

*   *   *   *   *

Silhouette Special Edition®

Now appearing
in a special return engagement, Nora Roberts's
bestselling 1988 miniseries featuring

THE O'HURLEYS!
Nora Roberts

Book 1 **THE LAST HONEST WOMAN** *Abby's Story*
Book 2 **DANCE TO THE PIPER** *Maddy's Story*
Book 3 **SKIN DEEP** *Chantel's Story*

And making his debut in a brand-new title, a very special
leading man . . . Trace O'Hurley!

Book 4 **WITHOUT A TRACE** *Trace's Tale*

In 1988, Nora Roberts introduced THE O'HURLEYS!—a close-knit
family of entertainers whose early travels spanned the country. The
beautiful triplet sisters and their mysterious brother each experience
the triumphant joy and passion only true love can bring, in four books
you will remember long after the last pages are turned.

Don't miss this captivating miniseries—a special collector's edition
available now wherever paperbacks are sold.

OHUR-1A

Win 1 of 10 Romantic Vacations and Earn Valuable Travel Coupons Worth up to $1,000!

Inside every Harlequin or Silhouette book during September, October and November, you will find a PASSPORT TO ROMANCE that could take you around the world.

By sending us the official entry form available at your favorite retail store, you will automatically be entered in the PASSPORT TO ROMANCE sweepstakes, which could win you a star-studded London Show Tour, a Carribean Cruise, a fabulous tour of France, a sun-drenched visit to Hawaii, a Mediterranean Cruise or a wander through Britain's historical castles. The more entry forms you send in, the better your chances of winning!

In addition to your chances of winning a fabulous vacation for two, valuable travel discounts on hotels, cruises, car rentals and restaurants can be yours by submitting an offer certificate (available at retail stores) properly completed with proofs-of-purchase from any specially marked PASSPORT TO ROMANCE Harlequin® or Silhouette® book. The more proofs-of-purchase you collect, the higher the value of travel coupons received!

For details on your PASSPORT TO ROMANCE, look for information at your favorite retail store or send a self-addressed stamped envelope to:

PASSPORT TO ROMANCE
P.O. Box 621
Fort Erie, Ontario L2A 5X3

ONE PROOF-OF-PURCHASE

3-CSIM-2

To collect your free coupon booklet you must include the necessary number of proofs-of-purchase with a properly completed offer certificate available in retail stores or from the above address.

© 1990 Harlequin Enterprises Limited